David Tetlow was born in Rossendale, Lancashire, during the Second World War. Following his school years, he worked in mechanical engineering and later joined the Lancashire Constabulary.

He is aware of ancestors who left Ireland around the mid-nineteenth century probably due to the famine, disease and poverty of those years to work in the construction industry and the then thriving textile mills in Lancashire.

As always to Joyce and my family, for their support.

David Tetlow

JOURNEY TO A NEW LIFE

AUSTIN MACAULEY PUBLISHERS™
LONDON • CAMBRIDGE • NEW YORK • SHARJAH

Copyright © David Tetlow 2023

The right of David Tetlow to be identified as author of this work has been asserted by the author in accordance with sections 77 and 78 of the Copyright, Designs and Patents Act 1988.

All rights reserved. No part of this publication may be reproduced, stored in a retrieval system, or transmitted in any form or by any means, electronic, mechanical, photocopying, recording, or otherwise, without the prior permission of the publishers.

Any person who commits any unauthorised act in relation to this publication may be liable to criminal prosecution and civil claims for damages.

This is a work of fiction. Names, characters, businesses, places, events, locales, and incidents are either the products of the author's imagination or used in a fictitious manner. Any resemblance to actual persons, living or dead, or actual events is purely coincidental.

A CIP catalogue record for this title is available from the British Library.

ISBN 9781398440869 (Paperback)
ISBN 9781398440876 (Hardback)
ISBN 9781398440883 (ePub e-book)

www.austinmacauley.com

First Published 2023
Austin Macauley Publishers Ltd®
1 Canada Square
Canary Wharf
London
E14 5AA

To David and Doreen Kettle. Bryan and Carol Lee for their very helpful knowledge of the area surrounding the Rivington Reservoirs, and to my Canadian daughter-in-law Sarah.

Chapter One

Liam Doyle had lived, for most of his life, in the small stone cottage in a wooded area close to Ballina in county Mayo Ireland. He was from a long line of stone masons, his grandfather Sean had built the cottage some sixty years before. He and his wife Sarah had moved in from the town after the premature death of his parents from typhus two years before. The year was 1848. Ireland was in the grip of the potato famine. Starvation and poverty had brought on the deadly diseases of typhus, cholera, and dysentery to the country. Many people were suffering, and the authorities appeared to care little about their plight.

The cottage was small and stone built when they moved in it comprising of only one room which was kitchen, lounge and bedroom. Liam had since built two small bedrooms to the side. They were a mile from the town and had no facilities. Water was taken from a nearby stream. Sarah insisted that it was always boiled on the peat fire before use.

The toilet was simply a trench dug into the outside ground with a wooden hut placed over it and a rough moveable toilet seat arranged over the trench. Whenever it was used, a shovel full of earth was thrown in and when eventually the trench was full, a new trench was dug and the hut and seat were moved a few yards. Simple but efficient. Friday evening was bath night when Liam used to take the tin bath hanging on the living room wall, filled it with warm water from the peat fire and taking turns to wash in the same water – youngest first.

The couple were now in their mid-thirties and had a son Connor and a daughter Hannah. Connor was eighteen and Hannah, sixteen. Because of Liam's skills the family had been faring better than most and he had begun to tutor Connor in the art of stone carving. Conditions in the county were quickly deteriorating; money was scarce and work for their craft was becoming much more difficult to find, and like many local families, they had entered upon hungry and arduous times.

Sarah at this time was their lifeline as she had managed to secure a position of a cook at the house of a local magistrate and landowner two miles from their home. She had to get to their manor house and start work at six every morning to cook breakfast for the Fitzsimons family which they would eat at eight. She then made them a packed lunch before travelling home, returning at five to cook dinner which she served at seven after which she was free to go home for the night. This she did seven days per week with no transport offered by the Fitzsimons and no time off.

When she began the job, she walked both-ways twice a day rain or shine – whatever the weather. Liam saw how her health was deteriorating from this effort and they were both aware this was the only thing which kept them healthy and indeed alive, putting a meagre amount of money in their pockets and food on their table at this time.

Some months before Liam's old friend Finn Kennedy, a local small holding farmer with less than one acre of land, had the gable end of his cottage collapse during a violent storm.

Finn and his wife Robyn were struggling for money and his landlord refused to pay for the repair. Liam and his son Connor had rebuilt the wall at no cost to the farmer or the landowner. He approached Finn and explained his wife's travelling difficulty.

They chatted. Finn said, 'Liam, look at my land. The crops are half of what it should be. They will barely feed me and my wife, and there won't be any to sell; if we stay here, we are going to go hungry this winter and I owe three months' rent which I haven't got. Because you repaired part of the house and there is a small crop to harvest. The landowner has given us three months to live here so long as we dig up and leave the potato crop behind and the cottage in good condition when we go.'

'Where will you go?'

'I hear that there is work for farm labourers in Lancashire and Cheshire England. We will sell what we can including the donkey and cart for the cost of travel. I hear that Liverpool people treat the Irish well and I should be able to find work. Anyway take Pat with you and use him and the jig as you wish until then.'

'Pat? Jig?'

'The donkey and cart you idiot.'

From that day on, Liam was able to transport his wife to and from her place of work in relative dryness and comfort.

Two weeks later, Liam and Connor found work repairing dry stone walls around a farmstead nine miles to the north of Ballina and reluctantly left Sarah and Hannah alone with Hannah in charge of Sarah's transport. 'We will be away for about three weeks; the farm is owned by John Gill, and it is near Stokane.'

Off went the thirty-eight-year-old slim, dark bearded, lithe and angular Liam Doyle, with his slim dark haired, handsome eighteen-year-old son glad to be working at long last and earning money to take care of the family and happy to be walking miles in order to do so.

It was Sunday afternoon; the walk to the farm carrying their tools with them would take about three hours. It was October and so the days were short. They would arrive a little before dark too far to return home each day. Liam told Connor that it was likely that they would sleep in the barn among the animals and work throughout the daylight hours each day until the job was done. As they walked, they talked.

'Dry stone wall repairing is a bit beneath you, Dad,' said Connor. 'You're a stone mason, you can carve stone beautifully and accurately for others to lay.'

'I'll take whatever I can get and be grateful for it. Dry stone wall building is quite an art. The walls have to stand whatever weather is thrown at them to last for hundreds of years; I can teach you these skills for the future.'

'What future, Dad? I love Ireland but the Irish people are starving and dying young from cholera and typhus – no one seems to care. We are lucky that we live in the countryside and away from the fevers and filth of the townships and that you and Ma can just about feed us. Look at Ma and Hannah, they dress every day in the same clothes. They can't afford anything new. We have to keep repairing and making do with the same shoes, boots and bedding because all we can do is feed ourselves and even then, we are hungry most of the time.'

'I have a few ideas about our future, and we can discuss those during the three weeks we will be together. The farmer John Gill has offered me twenty shillings a week and you as my labourer ten shillings a week wages, this will feed our family through some of the coming winter.'

They walked along and were still at least an hour from the farm when the weather changed and the wind and rain came. On arrival, the pair was soaked and very cold.

John Gill was a substantial and genial man, bald and with a heavy beard. He lived at the farm with his wife Emily and their three teenage daughters. To their surprise, he welcomed them into his home and gave them blankets while they stripped and dried themselves and their clothing in front of the open hearth.

'There will be a meal for you both in about one hour when your clothes are dry. In the meantime, I will tell you why I have hired you for three weeks. I have three miles of stone walls which have been neglected for years. I am a cattle and dairy farmer; the outer walls are very much in disrepair and if they are not fixed soon, I will be losing animals. The inner walls are completely down in places where my family and our labourers have climbed over them, broken them down and the weather has taken its toll. The cabin in the yard will be yours for the three weeks. It has a peat stove, water and two beds. You will take breakfast just before daylight in the house. My wife will provide you with packed lunches and your evening meal will be in the house at six. Any questions?'

'Yes Mr Gill,' said Liam.

'John please.'

'After we have eaten, can we get access to wood and tools? If the walls are completely down, we will need to make a couple of wooded frames to make sure that we build straight. We can do that tonight before we sleep.'

'Yes, there is a workshop next to the cabins with lanterns and tools.'

The steak meal made by Emily Gill was not only substantial but also delicious, particularly for two men who had rarely eaten steak and had been struggling to provide enough food for their family for years.

In the workshop, making the frames they would need later, Liam said to his son, 'I honestly thought that we would now be in the barn with the animals freezing cold, soaking wet and making do with the bit of bread and cheese we brought with us. We will work hard and do a damn good job for this lovely couple.'

The following morning after breakfast, John Gill announced, 'Right come on boys, I will take you round the walls and show what you are up against.'

A small pony and cart were outside awaiting them, and a tour of the farms extremities and inner walls revealed the work to be done. The farmer was correct; the walls were completely collapsed in places and the frames would be needed.

'Can you do it in three weeks?'

'It's a lot of work, but we should get around ten hours of daylight each day, let us hope for decent weather and, yes, we can do it,' replied Liam.

Chapter Two

Hannah Doyle Liam, Sarah's sixteen-year-old daughter, was given the responsibility of caring for Pat, the donkey which she took willingly and began to grow fond of the little animal and its peculiar quirks. Hannah was still a girl but growing rapidly into womanhood and was clearly even at that early stage going to be very beautiful, tall, slim with a pretty face. She had left school in the town two years before having learned basic mathematics and to speak Irish, English and some Mass Latin. She was the obvious daughter of her mother Sarah who was still a handsome woman but whose looks were beginning to fade, not because of her age but rather due to the long hours of work and the deprivation that the family were subjected to.

Life was a little easier now they had the donkey and cart temporarily. Hannah was driving her to work from home at five thirty every morning. Picking her up from the manor house at eleven after the packed lunches had been made and the kitchen thoroughly cleaned, then returning her to the house at four in the afternoon returning for her at nine when the family had been fed and the workplace scrubbed. This on every day of the week without any rest.

Sean Fitzsimons, a local magistrate, and his wife Mia – Sarah's employers were a hard task master and mistress. All their employees worked long hours without respite. If they were not up to the tasks given or became too sick to work, which under the circumstances of the time was a regular occurrence, they were immediately dismissed without money of reference or a thought given to their previous hard work and loyalty, or the suffering of their families.

Their son Darrah Fitzsimons was a large sour faced, spoiled and brutal man, unmarried at the age of twenty-four years and without any responsibility. He would harass and bully the workforce. If any retaliated, which they occasionally did, he would become petulant and demand that his father sack the unfortunate individual.

Sean Fitzsimons was also the owner of many of the local farms, both crop growing, sheep and dairy surrounding his manor into which he installed efficient farmers. The produce he sold at the highest price he could get without a thought to the countryside's ailing population. In fact, much of the yield went to the city's wealthier merchants or was transported abroad.

Sarah Doyle was aware of these things. She intensely disliked working for the family but felt that, at this time, she had no choice if she was to put food on the table back home. It was particularly repellent when, on occasions, Darrah Fitzsimons would burst into the kitchen when she was cooking the evening meal. He would lean against her from behind to see how much she would tolerate; she always quickly moved away.

On one occasion, he snatched a whole cooked chicken and walked off with it forcing her to start all over again. On this occasion, she prayed that she would soon be able to leave this dreadful family behind.

Having completed their first day's work, Liam and Connor were having another sumptuous meal with John Gill. After the meal they settled down for a short time in the kitchen and Liam said, 'John, may I ask a question without meaning to upset or annoy you?'

'Ask away,' John Gill said slightly bemused.

'While we worked today, we talked briefly with some of your farm labourers. They are very happy working for you I should say. But they told us that the local community around here are no better off than anywhere else in the county. They are hungry and disease is rife. Yet here we are amongst your animals and efficient farm. Can nothing be done for the local people?'

'Ah, Liam. You are under the mistaken impression that I own this farm. I wish that I did, and indeed if I did much of the stock would go out to the locals at prices they can afford. The farm is owned by a man who lives quite close to you in fact, a man called Sean Fitzsimons. Liam I am like you making a living for my family as best I can under these difficult times. I work hard as you do, and I create the produce, the meat, the milk, the butter and the cheese. The owner sells it. I have no idea of its destination. It is collected by his people and taken off. I simply earn my wages. I occasionally turn a blind eye and allow one of my labourers to sneak a side of beef into the village. If I am ever found out I will be sacked out of hand, so please don't ever say anything.'

'My apologies John, I obviously did not know that I will never mention this to anyone again. My wife works for the Fitzsimons, and I know what they are like.'

'In fact I have been meaning to tell you Liam that Fitzsimons' son Darrah sometimes appears here in horseback, sometimes alone and now and then with one of his mates. He is a big, dreadful ugly man who thinks he is god's gift to women, my daughters hide away when they get wind he is in the area. But don't tell him I said that. He may try to intimidate you. If he does and you retaliate, he will go crying to his dad and you will be sacked out of hand and without any pay. 'He's tried it with me in the past and I just say yes sir, no sir, three bags full sir. He gets fed up and goes away. I know that you are a proud man but, please don't take him on whatever he says.'

Liam looked purposely at his son and said, 'Don't worry John, we will ignore him.'

Chapter Three

On the Wednesday of the first week, her father and brother were away. Hannah was sitting on the cart outside the rear door of the manor awaiting her mother when she saw a large man, she assumed was Darrah Fitzsimons from the description given to her by the mother, on horseback riding towards the stables which brought him alongside of her. He stopped.

'Not seen you here before pretty girl, who are you?'

'Hannah Doyle. I'm here to pick up my mother.'

'Ah, your mother's our cook, didn't know her name, she travels in style eh with that donkey and battered old cart.'

At that and to Hannah's relief, he rode off towards the stables. Her mother came out a few minutes later. As they rode home the weather was fine, and Sarah was enjoying the views. As they approached their cottage she looked behind and saw a rider. 'That looks like Darrah Fitzsimons I hope he's not following us.

'He spoke to me outside the kitchen door a few minutes ago.'

'Let's go inside,' she shouted so that Fitzsimons could hear. 'Liam and Connor, we are home.'

As they did so Sarah glanced back and saw Fitzsimons look at her, then ride away.

'They are not here Ma.'

'You know that. I know that he does not. Listen to me carefully Hannah, that man is bad news. Don't give him any encouragement at all.'

'Don't worry Ma.' She laughed. 'He's too old, too fat and too ugly for my taste,' she said flippantly.

'I mean it, we are on our own here for the next two and a half weeks. If he gets to know that he will try it on, you are starting to look like a young woman now, please don't take any risks.'

They agreed that Hannah would in future drive up to the kitchen door a few minutes after eleven so that she would not have to wait and attract his attention. She did this the following day and as she drew up, Sarah immediately walked to her and began to alight the cart. Before they could set off, Darrah Fitzsimons walked towards them and shouted, 'Stop there.'

He had one arm behind his back and as he approached from behind, he investigated the rear of the cart, bent forward and appeared to produce a small paper parcel from the cart.

'Ah. I knew that there was some thieving going on.' He threw the parcel onto Sarah's lap. 'What have you to say about that? No never mind I now know that you're a thief and I will bear it in mind for the future. I'll let you off this time, but don't forget that you are both in my debt.' He was wearing gloves and he thumped the cart with his fist fracturing one of the thin wooden struts.

At that he walked off. Sarah opened the parcel and saw that it contained the rotting remains of the chicken he had taken from the kitchen a few days before.

On their way home, Sarah said, 'He is clearly as stupid as he is repellent, but now we know that we also know how careful we have to be. I think that he will leave us alone so long as he thinks your Dad and Connor are at home.'

As the wall builders worked, Liam taught Connor the rudiments of dry-stone walling. First moving the fallen coping stones away for later. Checking that the foundations were still in place and straight and building layer upon layer of stones of similar width, and occasionally anchoring them with larger stones for stability and when the correct height had been reached, finishing with the half rounded coping stones. Occasionally they found that coping stones were missing, and new ones had to be created – an ideal opportunity for Connor to learn a little of the skills of the stone mason. Hard backbreaking work. No problem to Liam who was used to it and Connor was also beginning to be so.

As they worked they talked, and Liam began to talk about his long-term dream for the family, 'When we get enough money together, I want first to get your mother out of the soul-destroying job she is in and the four of us catch a steamship from Sligo to Liverpool in England. Then one of the big ships to Canada or America which I am told are the lands of great opportunities for people like us who are not afraid of hard work.'

Emily Gill had taken to the two, her three teenage daughters. Rather than making their packed lunch to take with them after breakfast she, or one of the girls would find them in the meadows at lunchtime with sandwiches and milk for a chat which the men also enjoyed. Particularly Connor who had become smitten by the seventeen-year-old Emelia, a lovely young woman with freckles and beautiful red hair.

On the Thursday of their first week at the farm, Emelia came to find them at lunchtime with lovely cheese sandwiches, thick with butter, and milk still slightly warm from the cow. 'I've been given some time off work to look after you,' she spoke.

She began to tell him of her life. Up at the crack of dawn and into the cow shed with her sisters and other young women from the village with fifty head of cattle to milk. Then into the creamery where they were employed endlessly stirring vats of milk to produce butter and cheese. 'Would you like to see inside the creamery? I'll take you if you want.'

'Dad, can I have a couple of hours off to look round the farm?'

'Aye course you can, but two hours only mind.'

Connor and Emelia went joyfully, happy in each other's company. It was a fifteen-minute walk to the creamery. A huge wooden barn, where he saw the many vats being manually stirred by farm workers. He thought that it looked easier than wall building until he was given a huge ladle at Emelia's instigation. After twenty minutes, he was more than happy to return it.

'I've often wondered,' he spoke. 'Do cows just eat grass to give milk?'

'No of course they don't silly, they have to have a calf every year to produce milk, that's why we have to keep a good bull. You don't know much about farming, do you?'

'You mean one bull is the—' he pondered how to phrase it. 'The husband to all these cows.'

'Yes.'

'Lucky bull.'

'Do you have to milk them every day?'

'We milk them twice a day and some cows need milking a third time a few days after calving.'

'We've just time to visit the abattoir before you go back,' she spoke. 'I'll show you some bullocks that aren't so lucky.'

'Is that where they kill the animals?'

'Yes. You'll find it very interesting. Dairy and beef production is what this farm is about.'

Connor Doyle knew that he was slightly squeamish when it came to matters connected with blood, if he or anyone else in his eyeshot cut their hands or any other part of them, he felt sick and slightly dizzy. 'I'll give that one a miss.'

'Oh come on, it's part of life, you eat meat, we all eat meat, why not see where it comes from.'

Despite his reluctance and so as not to seem cowardly and to please this young lady, he entered the abattoir. He immediately saw a young bullock with its head forcibly held high between two wooden posts with its back legs tied with rope. He saw a huge man with what at first looked like a sledgehammer, but as he looked again, he saw that it had a six-inch-long spike on one side.

She said, to warn Connor, 'He will kill it with one stroke, he is very good at his job. Then they will haul it up by the back legs and slit its belly and the guts will tumble out and …'

At that Connor ran. He shouted, 'Dad will be waiting for me, and I'll be in trouble if I don't get back.'

His growing feelings for the lovely young girl he had left behind had for now, completely evaporated.

Liam laughed when Connor told him the story. 'You used to almost faint whenever you saw your mother skin a rabbit, but you never left a bit on your plate later. The girl is fine she has lived with the life and death of animals all her life, it's you, you dope who have never had to deal with this before.'

Later that day, Connor realised that she was only giving him a warning of what was to come and his warm feelings for this lovely young girl came back to him stronger than ever.

Chapter Four

On the Thursday morning of their final drystone walling three weekly slog, Liam and Connor were slowing down a little, the job was almost done, and they wanted to ensure that they received the full three weeks wages due to them before they left on the Friday evening.

Sarah and Hannah were also feeling relieved that the men would be home soon. They had been very worried about Darrah Fitzsimons and his potential threat to Sarah's livelihood and Hannah's safety but were reassured in the thought that he believed the men were at home.

That lunchtime Liam and Connor expected, as usual that one of the ladies would bring out their lunch. They were working quite close to the farmhouse and John Gill walked across with their packed lunches. 'Thanks John, very kind, you must be having a quiet day, it's normally your wife or one of your girls who brings out the food.'

'No Liam it's not that. We are due a visit today from the boss's son Darrah. A bloody idiot who thinks he knows it all. He comes pretending to crack the whip, ordering folk about. If anyone has a go back, he will fire them off without wages. My advice to you if he comes near is to say nothing like I told you before, "Yes sir, no sir, three bags full sir."'

'What about your wife and girls?'

'Oh, they are frightened to death of him. They always hide whenever he is about. We won't see any of them until he has gone, he'll try to rub up against them or maul them if he gets half a chance.'

'Why do you put up with that John?'

'Liam, you know well why I put up with it, to make a decent living in these hard times. The same reason you are rebuilding these walls.'

Later that afternoon, they were working about fifty yards from the farmhouse when they both saw a large man on horseback ride up and tie his horse to a farm gate. He walked inside without bothering to knock and even from so far away they could hear his loud shouting, clearly making his unruly presence felt.

Eventually, he walked from the house followed by John Gill shouting, 'Why are they away? I wanted a chat with your lovely daughters and something good to eat, that's why I came here, not for your bloody company and you tell me they have all gone out shopping. Not good enough, Gill.'

'I'll make you something.'

'I'd rather eat cow shit than your food, who are those two over there? Not seen them before.'

'Just two outside labourers rebuilding the walls.'

'Shoddy bloody job with the looks of it.' In an angry mood he strode towards them.

'If you are employed by me to do a job, at least do it properly,' he shouted as he approached.

Fitzsimons walked to a section of the newly, and very well-built wall and attempted to push a section of it down from the middle, pushing at it with his shoulders. He was unable to; he did not have the strength and it would not move and he became breathless and irritated with the effort. He was forced angrily and eventually to push half a dozen coping stones from the top and he did not find that easy, still panting sweating and shouting. 'Look, rubbish like I said.' He obviously did not have either the intelligence or the gumption to feel even slightly embarrassed at his own crass stupidity.

'Who are you two anyway?'

'Just labourers for your dad.'

That appeared to anger him even more. 'You had better remember that you work for me, if I fire you off, you're gone. I said who are you, what's your names?'

Connor could see that his father was reluctant to even speak to this ignorant man so he said, 'I'm Connor Doyle and this is my dad, Liam.'

Light appeared to ignite even in this man's dull eyes. 'Are you from near Ballina?'

'Yes why?'

'Does your mother work at the manor as a cook?'

'Yes.'

'She's a thief I caught her stealing from the kitchen the other day and out of the goodness of my heart, I let her off. You have a sister called Hannah, don't you?'

Liam became animated at that remark and snapped. 'How do you know Hannah?'

Fitzsimons gave a huge smile, turned, and walked off towards his horse, as he got to it, he mounted and laughing loudly he rode off back towards Ballina.

As he rode, he howled with pleasure at what he was about to do gulping at the powerful poteen he had hidden in his saddle bag.

Liam's heart sank. 'John by the time he gets back, Sarah will be at the manor and Hannah will be home on her own. Should I be worried?'

John Gill replied, 'Liam from what I have just heard and knowing that beast as I do, yes you should.'

'Will you take us back home now on your cart?'

'Gladly, if I could. But the girls have it and I don't know when they will be back.'

Connor shouted, 'Dad I can run home in just over an hour from here. Don't worry if he's there I will look after her.'

At that he ran off without looking back leaving Liam staring helplessly.

'Liam,' John said. 'The cart should be back within the next half hour before it goes dark as soon as it arrives, I will take you home, please do your best not to worry.'

Connor knowing that he had nine miles to run eased his pace to stay the distance. It started to go dark, but luckily there were few clouds and a moon to keep him from blundering into the ditches. He ran on steadily and sure enough just over an hour later he approached home.

To his horror, at the beginning of the track to their cottage he saw Fitzsimons's horse tied to a tree. As he got nearer, he could hear a man's voice shouting, 'You know you want this and it will keep your Ma out of trouble.' The man laughed, then he heard the voice of his sister screaming and crying in fear. Connor, exhausted from his run pushed at the door, found it unlocked and ran inside. He saw Fitzsimons who had Hannah pinned in a corner and was trying to kiss her, tearing at her dress at the same time.

'Get off her you bastard,' he shouted.

Fitzsimons turned to see the tired breathless smaller man standing in front of him. 'You got here quick,' he shouted as he hit Connor in the face hard with his first. Connor staggered and tried to fight back but was unable to avoid the following blows which exploded into his face and body. Hannah attacked from behind but was unable to stop the punishment to her brother.

Fitzsimons eventually threw the unconscious Connor out through the door and locked it with the bar.

'Now, where were we before we were interrupted?'

Moments later, Connor came slowly around and could still hear the shouting and screaming. He again tried the door but this time found it locked. He knew of a faulty catch on his bedroom window through which he had entered the cottage quietly on several occasions. He went to the side and climbed through. As he passed his bed, he picked up a heavy chamber pot.

Connor went quietly into the living room where to his distress he saw that Fitzsimons had stripped his sister of all her clothes and was tugging frantically at his own trousers as he held her helplessly in the corner. Connor crept close and using both hands, he hit Fitzsimmons as hard as he could on the back of his head with the underside of the heavy pot. He heard a crack and Fitzsimons immediately collapsed to the floor.

Liam and John Gill had set off in the cart from the farm half an hour behind Connor, but the fit draught horse was able to trot at a good pace and when they reached the cottage, they were only fifteen minutes behind Connor.

As Connor, they were both horrified to see Fitzsimons' horse and together they ran to the cottage.

What they saw there would stay in Liam's mind for the rest of his life. His daughter wrapped in a blanket, being held close by his son in a corner of the room. Both clearly in shock, with bruised and swollen faces, staring into space with tears rolling down their cheeks and with the huge prostrate body of Darrah Fitzsimons lying at their feet with his poteen bottle by his side.

It took a moment for them to realise that their father was in the room. Liam's mouth hung open aghast. 'What?'

'He tried to rape me, Dad, he beat Connor up and tried to rape me, he would not stop.'

'Tried to rape you,' Liam spluttered.

'He didn't succeed Dad.'

'Thank God.'

'I had to hit him to get him off. I think I've killed him.'

The family stared at each other in stunned silence. John Gill was the first to recover. He knelt by the huge Bulk. 'No, he's not dead, his breathing is pretty strong. His hair is matted with blood. I think he's in a bad way, may have a cracked skull, but he's not dead.'

'What do we do now?' said Liam.

At those words there was a deathly silence no one spoke, and the air was heavy with fearful thought.

John eventually said, 'Liam. I know the Fitzsimons family; I've worked for them for a long time. They are the most dreadful, vengeful people I have ever come across. If he dies, Sean Fitzsimons will want your son's head in a noose and he will strive very hard to get that and with his connections, he may well succeed. If he lives, they will concoct stories and lies which will condemn you, your wife, your son and daughter. Even if they cannot prove anything against you, they will make certain that none of you will ever find work again. He'll starve you to death. Believe me you need to get away where he can't possibly find you.'

The shock over and reality setting in, Liam's mind began to work overtime.

Sarah will leave the manor about eight o'clock. I have always planned to leave here with my family eventually, it now seems that we will be leaving sooner rather than later. Will you help us John? Your horse and cart are outside, and we will need some transport for a while?'

'Yes. I've grown very fond of you and your son, but you may never speak of my help, or I and my family will follow you into exile or starvation.'

At seven-thirty. Using the donkey and small cart, Connor and Hannah set off to the manor to collect their mother. John and Liam led Fitzsimons' horse with Darrah Fitzsimons slumped unconscious on its back and followed them.

Just beyond the front gate of the manor Liam was aware there was a stone mounting block with no one around, they lowered him from the horse as gently as they could and placed him on the ground with his back leaning against the block. The remains of the poteen were poured by Liam around his mouth and neck and placed the empty bottle in his right hand. He then wrapped the horses rein around Fitzsimons' left wrist with the animal anchored to its master. They left him and returned to the cottage.

Sarah, her son, and daughter arrived back a little after them having left the manor by the rear gate. Sarah was dumbfounded when the events of the past hours were related to her. The family, now including John Gill, sat to discuss their future. If indeed they had any.

Liam and Sarah had always intended eventually to leave Ireland but not until they had the funds and wherewithal to settle elsewhere. It now seemed that they had no choice but to leave this beautiful part of the world because of hunger, disease, and the possibility of reprisals from the Fitzsimons family.

John Gill spoke, 'It's more of a likelihood than a possibility. He will, I am sure, wake up one day soon and remember. It's up to you, I have your wages at the farm that should pay your passage with a bit spare.'

Connor who was still hurting badly said, 'We should have killed him while we had the chance.'

'That's not who we are Connor, and you know it,' Liam snapped reprovingly.

The family began their hurried preparations to leave Ireland for ever, packing they're meagre possessions and into bags which could easily be carried, their intention being the make for the port at Sligo and cross the Irish sea to Liverpool in England, then what, none of them knew…

'Before we leave, we must return Finn and Robyn's donkey and cart,' said Sarah. 'We can't take that with us, and we can't leave it here.'

Liam made a mental note. It was late in November, cold and drizzling with rain, when they were wrapped up well as could be, ready to go and with tears and great emotion they left their cottage behind and set off in the two carts.

The Finns' cottage was on the way. Liam's intention was not to involve their good friends in the escapade and simply to leave the donkey and cart tied outside for them to find in the morning. Sarah however said, 'Liam, they are our best friends, we have known them all our lives. We cannot leave without saying goodbye.'

It was eleven in the evening. Finn and Robyn were fast asleep in their bed when the banging on the door came. 'What the ...' shouted Finn, 'I hope it's not who I think it is.'

He opened the door and was greatly relieved to see Liam and Sarah but was bewildered to see his son and daughter together with a man he knew slightly, a fellow farmer John Gill.

Sarah spoke first, 'Robyn, Finn we have come to say goodbye.'

She went on to explain fully what had happened to bring them to his point, after which Finn said, 'Give us one minute.' And he and Robyn went into the bedroom. They were back within seconds.

Finn spoke to John, 'Will you buy the donkey and cart from me?'

John Gill thought quickly. 'Yes, they will be useful to my girls, they are always borrowing my horse and cart to go shopping.'

'Liam, Sarah. You may not know but Darrah Fitzsimons owns this small farm, it was given to him by his father a few months ago. He is here most days bullying and trying it on with Robyn, she's scared to death of him, and we will both be delighted to get away from here and him. Let him dig his own bloody spuds up. We are coming with you. Give us ten minutes to get ready.'

'Are you sure?' said Liam, 'we don't know what the future holds, we may climb out of the hot water and into the inferno.'

'Whatever happens, it's our choice and we are coming with you.'

The group set off on their unchartered odyssey with John and Finn driving the two carts along the cold, damp road back to the farm where John gently awakened Emily and unfolded the situation.

She, Sarah, and Robyn went to the kitchen where they wrapped food and drinks for the journey ahead. Emily had never met the other women before, but they all got along as if they had been long term friends. At the conclusion she remarked, 'In many ways I wish that we were travelling with you. I would be very happy to get well away from the dreadful Fitzsimons family.'

Whilst Connor and Hannah snoozed in the hall, John paid Liam and Finn. Liam received ninety shillings for the wall repairs while Finn received a generous forty shillings for the elderly donkey and the cart which needed extensive repair. They were both delighted with the money.

They woke Connor and Hannah. Before they left, Connor said to John, 'Can I speak to Emelia before we go, just to say goodbye.'

'No I'm sorry Connor, she is fast asleep now. It upset her greatly when you ran from her the last time you were together, the bullocks must be killed for beef and she does her best to see that it is done as quickly and humanly as possible. She has now got over that and I don't want to upset her again.'

John Gill then took charge of the situation. 'The six of you now lie in the bottom of my cart. I am going to cover you with hay to make the journey look more normal and to keep some of the rain off you. I suggest that you eat something then sleep. I will take you along the coast lanes to about five miles from

Sligo harbour. It will take a few hours. When I drop you off, I will return home and none of this ever happened. I beg each of you never to mention my involvement in this ever again or my life and that of my family will be in danger.'

The six, who trusted John implicitly and were generally exhausted did as they were bid to do and found that under the hay, they were comfortable and warm and slept. They did not know for how long until they were awakened by their driver. It was early morning, just starting to come light on the last day of November. They were aware that the cart had come to a stop.

'Please stay where you are for a few more minutes. You are about four or five miles from Sligo harbour, it's downhill all the way. When you get out of the cart you will realise that you are not alone. There are dozens of people walking that way, so I guess that there must be a ship leaving today. I have been here before loading cattle onto the ships and I know that you will have competition to get aboard. I suggest that you join the queue immediately you get down there. The very best of luck to you all. As soon as you are out, I am turning and leaving. I don't want anyone to recognise me. Ok, please go.'

John Gill watched all six alight from the cart and as soon as they had collected their baggage, he immediately set off back without saying goodbye or even looking in their direction.

Chapter Five

Willey Baird, Darrah Fitzsimons's groom had been sitting and trying to keep himself awake all that same night in the stables of the Fitzsimons manor awaiting the return of Darrah. He dare not take to his bed until Cable, the horse of his master, had been brushed, fed, watered, and bedded down for the night and the saddle and reins cleaned and polished. His livelihood was at stake if he was not at the back and call of Fitzsimons on his return to the stables. Darrah Fitzsimons had, on many occasions, stayed out all night without informing his groom and the situation although exhausting was not unusual.

At seven o'clock, Pat O'Shaughnessy, the other groom, walked into the stables and on seeing the tiredness of Baird, the empty loose box and realising immediately his predicament said, 'Ok Willey off you go, if he comes in this morning I will see to him, get yourself to bed.'

With great relief, Willey Baird decided to have a breath of fresh air before hitting the hay. He walked into the garden at the side of the manor house, musing to himself, if *I could only find myself the same job with another family, I would jump at it.*

It was beginning to come daylight and he could see towards the front driveway of the manor and in the distance, he saw a horse standing still with its head down. 'Cable?' he said out loud. Willey knew that he, as a lowly groom, was not allowed on the front driveway unless he was ordered to be there. However at that time on a wet November morning, he knew that he would not be seen.

He set off to retrieve the horse and take it to the stables, assuming that it had been abandoned there by its drunken master. *A new low even for him,* he thought.

As he approached, he saw that Darrah Fitzsimons was in fact with his horse lying at its feet with his head at an angle against the mounting block with his legs splayed apart. Willey had a sudden, hard to resist urge to kick Fitzsimons in the crotch. He did not succumb but rather knelt by his boss, smelled the strong alcohol aroma, and could hear from deep-within snoring and something which sounded like a deep throated moan. 'If I can get him to bed without anyone else knowing I could maybe earn some good points. Unlikely but worth a try.'

With difficulty, he pulled Fitzsimmons into a sitting position against the block. Fitzsimons head flopped forward and Willey immediately saw the blood at the back of his head. He lowered him back onto the block. Fitzsimons head flopped back onto the block with a dull thud. 'Oops,' said Willey.

Leaving everything as it had been, Willey ran to the rear door of the manor, even in an emergency he would not approach the front door. As he went into the kitchen, he expected to see Sarah Doyle. There was no one there. He ran through to the house not sure which way to go; he had never been in the house before. He found himself at the foot a grand staircase.

He was wondering what to do next when he saw Mr O'Brien, the butler, walking down the stairs towards him. 'What the hell are you doing there Willey, get the hell out of here before you get into serious trouble.'

'It's Darrah Fitzsimons. He's unconscious and injured near the front mounting block. He needs help.'

'Is he drunk?'

'I think so but I could not wake him up.'

They went outside together. It was the first time in Willey's ten years at the manor that he had been allowed through the front door. O'Brien looked down on Darrah. 'I thought so, drunk, fallen from his horse and cracked his head on the block. Find something we can use as a stretcher, and we will get him to his bed. Bring Pat, it will take the three of us to lift him.'

Willey and Pat came to the block with an old door and some horse blankets, and the three strong men carried him with great difficulty to his bedroom where they stripped him and put him to bed with a towel at the back of his head to stem the bleeding.

'Ok. You two had better hop it while I inform Mr Fitzsimons.'

'By the way Mr O'Brien, where is Mrs Doyle. I thought that she would be cooking breakfast about now?' O'Brien frowned slightly puzzled. 'She should be there.'

Downstairs there was no one around, so Willey and Pat nudged each other mischievously and went out through the front door to retrieve the horse, giggling like two overgrown schoolboys.

O'Brien checked the kitchen before reporting to Fitzsimons, and sure enough there was no activity.

He knocked nervously on Fitzsimons's bedroom door to find Sean Fitzsimons sat up in bed. 'What are you doing here O'Brien I expected Doyle with my breakfast?'

'Two things sir. We have just put young Mr Fitzsimons to bed. We found him asleep outside. It looked as if he had fallen from his horse and banged his head?'

'Drunk, of course.'

'Very likely sir.'

'Ok, you have told me. He'll sleep it off. Now send Doyle up with my breakfast.'

'That's the other thing sir. She's not there.'

'Not there,' he exploded.

'Not there.'

'Where the hell is she?'

'I don't know sir.'

'Don't know, don't know, you bloody well should know. Cook me a breakfast now, then find me a new cook before tomorrow morning. She's fired. Oh and you had better pop next door and tell his mother. Cook her breakfast as well.'

On his way to the kitchen O'Brien could see himself becoming butler and kitchen cook for the foreseeable future. A situation he dreaded. As he passed through the hall, he saw Sadie Baird, Willey's wife who was the house cleaner at work. 'Mrs Baird, can you cook?'

'Of course I can, Mr O'Brien.'

'Ah, problem solved.'

Chapter Six

The intrepid six began the trek towards Sligo harbour and as they walked, they became aware of just how fortunate they were, they were all in reasonable health, had eaten and slept, were warmly dressed and ready to face the walk.

They had joined dozens of others walking towards the docks and it was obvious how malnourished and sick many of the others were, driven by the likelihood of work in the thriving Lancashire cotton mills or the lure of further transport to the rapidly expanding countries of Canada or the United States. It was still cold and drizzling with rain and many were ill dressed limping and wet through and suffering, obviously having walked all night towards their hopeful destination and salvation.

Without wishing to consciously take advantage of their relative well-being, they found that they were walking considerably quicker than most others. News travels and as they spoke with others, they became aware that the Steamship SS Londonderry was in the harbour and would sail for Liverpool later that same day.

This news made them quicken their pace and one and a half hours after being dropped off by Gill they approached the berth as did many others. Finn shouted, 'Let's get a move on.'

He and Robyn ran forward to join the queue. Sarah tripped over a flagstone and had to be helped to her feet by Liam and a family of four beat them to the rear of the queue.

Finn looked back and shouted, 'we'll come back to you.'

'No,' replied Liam. 'Stay where you are, hopefully we'll all get aboard.'

They stood in the queue shivering and wet for three hours whilst first class passengers, animals and goods were loaded. Eventually the queue began to move forward, and people began to climb up the ramp onto the ship. There appeared to be hundreds of people before them, and the movement was slow. However slowly those waiting in front of them shrank and they saw Finn and Robyn give their names to the steward and walk up the ramp.

Liam's heart sank to his boots when the steward then pointed to the four in front of them and shouted, 'You're the last four.'

Father and Mother and two small boys walked forward and began to give their names. When the steward said, 'Stop, look at his legs.' He pointed to one of the boys, from where he stood Liam could see liquid excrement running freely down the boy's legs. 'He has dysentery, you can't bring him aboard.'

His mother began to cry, 'It's only a bit of diarrhoea. I'll clean him up. He's fine, please let us get on the ship.'

'See the harbour doctor. If he gives the Ok, you can wait for another ship. I can't let you aboard. Now move away. You four names?'

Feeling deep sorrow for the other family and at the same time great relief for themselves they gave their names and were allowed aboard.

It was late afternoon in the Fitzsimons manor and Mia Fitzsimons was visiting her son in his bedroom. He still appeared to be sleeping off his drunken fall, but she was getting worried. Speaking to her husband downstairs she said, 'I can't wake him no matter how I try. He needs a doctor.'

'What, it will cost a fortune just to wake the drunken idiot.'

'I really think that he has badly damaged himself in the fall, we definitely need a doctor. If you don't send for one and he dies. I will never let you have another peaceful moment for the rest of our time together.'

Sean Fitzsimons was a harsh and nasty man but even he knew when to draw the line, he sent a carriage for Doctor Malone in Ballina. The doctor arrived an hour and a half later and spent some time with their son. His verdict was that Darrah had fractured his skull when he fell from the animal. He had tightly bandaged the injury.

'He is likely to make a recovery, there has been no leakage other than blood from the injury and the skull seems stable. I will be back tomorrow morning to check the bandaging. If he should call out during the night, don't worry it may be that he is remembering and that is a good sign.'

Sean Fitzsimons woke from his dreams at three in the morning, wondering at first what had awakened him. Then he heard shouting from his son's bedroom. He pressed the button summoning O'Brien from his sleep.

'O'Brien, go and sit with him and see what he is shouting about. Let me know in the morning. Off you go, and don't forget my breakfast.'

Later that morning while Fitzsimons was eating his breakfast cooked by Mrs Baird, O'Brien, now dressed and reasonably responsive, attended him.

'I sat with Mr Darrah for about an hour until he settled. He was shouting something that sounded like Doyle. Doyle. That went on for a while, he must have shouted that name twenty or more times. Then he swore.'

'Go on.'

He shouted, 'Doyle, get away you little bastard I am busy with this bitch.

'While he shouted that he was thrashing about as though he was fighting.'

'That's strange,' said Fitzsimons. 'Do you think this has something to do with the Doyle woman who worked in our kitchen?'

'I could not possible say sir.'

'Go and see her this morning, let's hear what she has to say.'

O'Brien took the carriage. He had to go to Ballina to collect the doctor later that morning, so he called at the Doyle cottage on the way. Knocking on the door brought no response. He tried the door which to his surprise was unlocked and he entered. There was of course no one home. He looked around and was a little surprised at the absence of personal items, he could not see any coats, trousers, or dresses.

He was about to leave when he saw stains on the stone flag floor in the corner of the living kitchen. He dabbed at the stains with his white handkerchief and saw that they were red in colour. 'Blood?' he said to himself.

Carrying on with his journey he picked up the good doctor from his home and returned to the manor. Doctor Malone checked his dressings from the previous day and was happy with them. 'The less that we interfere with them the quicker the fracture will heal,' he said to the assembled company of Sean and Mia Fitzsimons and O'Brien. 'Open the curtains, let the light shine in maybe it will awaken him.'

O'Brien opened the curtains and the bright sunlight shone into the room. Almost immediately, Darrah Fitzsimons' eyes began to move under his closed eyelids. 'Yes, it looks to me as though he is about to wake up. I must warn you he may not make any sense if he awakens,' said the doctor.

As they waited, Sean Fitzsimons said to O'Brien, 'Did you find out anything from the Doyle family?'

'Not from the family sir, no. It looks like they have left the area completely, I could find no trace of them. I did however find traces of what looked like blood in a corner of the living room.' He produced the handkerchief.

The doctor examined it and spoke, 'Indeed that is blood.'

Darrah Fitzsimons groaned, and his eyes opened briefly. 'Doyle,' he shouted, 'Doyle hit me.' His eyes closed and he fell back into his deep sleep.

'It looks like he will make a full recovery. Keep him in bed for two weeks to allow the fracture to mend and he should be as good as new. Send for me if you need me.'

'I want you back here tomorrow.'

'I don't have the time, there is too much sickness and hunger in the town. I have been meaning to ask you again to spare some grain and meat from your farms for the poor townspeople, they need it badly.'

'Doctor, I've told you a dozen times before, my produce goes to those who can afford to pay for it.'

'O'Brien, take Doctor Malone home, I will come with you. I want to speak to Sergeant O'Keeffe at the police station.'

On the way to Ballina, Malone and Fitzsimons were silent and obviously not happy in the company of each other. O'Brien said, 'I was talking to Mrs Baird this morning and she tells me that she was friendly with Sarah Doyle and was told during one of their conversations that the Doyle's intend to move away from Ireland at some point, I'm beginning to think that what they have done.'

'What, without giving me notice, stupid woman, even more evidence if it was needed that the Doyle's have assaulted my son,' said Fitzsimons.

At the police station they found that O'Keeffe was off duty and at home; without waiting for a reply to his knocking, Fitzsimons walked into the house shouting, 'O'Keeffe, where are you?'

The off-duty sergeant walked through from the kitchen snarling and looking very annoyed until he saw Fitzsimons, he attempted a smile which looked more like a grimace saying, 'Ah Mr Fitzsimons, what can I do for you sir?'

'My son has been assaulted by a member of the Doyle family. He was almost killed and is severely injured with a fractured skull. It looks like they are trying to escape by leaving Ireland. The nearest port is Sligo. I want you and one of your constables off to Sligo right now. You know them by sight, if you see them on the road or at the port you will pick them up and bring the whole family back here to face my justice.'

'O'Keeffe thought, *I would happily almost kill the bastard myself,* but said. 'I will happily do as you say sir, but I don't have any transport.'

'Come back to the manor with us and you can take my horse and carriage. I want those Doyle's back here and incarcerated in your cells.'

An hour later Sergeant O'Keeffe and Constable Riley left the manor house. Riley driving in the cold drizzling rain and O'Keeffe sat in the back wrapped in his great coat travelling in grand style.

He began to muse about Sean Fitzsimons. He was a magistrate appointed by the county and supposed to act in the courthouse in a fair and impartial manner. He did anything but that. The sons or daughters of anyone influential in the county almost inevitably were found not guilty of crimes which often amounted to assaulting their servants or people they regarded as of the lower order, whether the allegations be of a sexual nature or of causing injury. People of that so-called lower order were rarely found not guilty and often received punishment far exceeding the crime. O'Keefe had often suspected Darrah Fitzsimons of several similar offences, but no one had ever made a complaint.

On the other hand, he had the greatest respect for the Doyle family, they had, so far as he was aware, never caused any offence to anyone.

Chapter Seven

SS Londonderry set off from Sligo into the North Atlantic Ocean for the two-day voyage with one hundred and seventy steerage passengers aboard the ship. It was the intention of the Captain Alexander Johnson to steam around the northern tip of Ireland and call in at the port of Derry for further supplies.

As they left Sligo, most of the passengers including the Doyle's found a place in the open air where they would be forced to endure the cold and wet weather rather than go below where the filth and stench of animals was unbearable.

As the ship got into the open sea, strong winds started to blow and indications were that it would become a very heavy storm. The captain ordered the ship's company to place all steerage passengers in an empty aft storage space to weather the approaching storm.

The storage space which was vile and stinking was eighteen feet long by twelve feet wide and the crew forced all one hundred and seventy men, women and children into that space where there was standing room only. The Doyle's were one of the last families in and were standing close to a wall and the only ladder available.

To cheer themselves up despite their dreadful predicament, the passengers began to sing one of the old songs.

> In Derry Vale beside the singing river,
> so oft I strayed, ah many years ago,
> and culled at morn the golden daffodillies
> that came with spring to set the world aglow.

As the storm grew worse, rain and salt water poured onto the passengers who were beginning to be thrown about by the increasing violent movement of the ship, the singing stopped. Some of the children and more elderly people were slipping and falling to the floor and finding it impossible to get back up because of the pressure of bodies and had to lay where they fell.

Liam Doyle was finding their treatment completely unacceptable and climbed the ladder intending to complain to the captain who saw him emerge from the storage area and heard him shout those conditions below were dreadful and people were falling and getting soaked with rain and sea water. Without listening to him further, the captain ordered his men to push Doyle back into the storage area and place the wood and tarpaulin hatch cover over the area and lock it down to prevent any further intervention.

The one hundred and seventy people were now in complete darkness. The floor was already wet with water and people were being sick adding to the slippery surface. The full force of the storm now hit the ship which rocked violently from side to side throwing people to the deck with others falling on top of them. Liam and Connor Doyle held their two women against the ladder with their arms locked together to prevent them from falling. The noise of shouting crying and screaming was carrying to the ship's crew.

Unimaginably worse was yet to come. The wood and tarpaulin hatch cover was now preventing oxygen from getting into the hold and all the passengers began to gasp for air and the noise from them subsided, deluding the ship's crew into thinking that all was well when in fact people were lying some on top of others and beginning to die from oxygen starvation.

Liam, who had his basic tool kit with him again climbed the ladder and with a hammer and chisel knocked a hole in the hatch cover to allow at least a little air into the hold. Two crew members assumed that he was trying to break out and stood ready to push him back.

Hours later, the ship docked at the Port of Derry in Loch Foyle and the hatch was removed. The scene was devastating, passengers were locked together in groups with their faces blackened and distorted by convulsions. Some were bruised and bleeding from their desperate struggle to stay alive. Of the one hundred and seventy people who were forced into the hold, seventy-two men women and children were dead.

At about this time Sergeant O'Keeffe and Constable Riley arrived at the port of Sligo and made their way to the office of the Harbour Master. They were informed that the ship SS Londonderry had left the port some hours before. It was confirmed that a family by the name of Doyle had been aboard at the time of departure.

'I'm glad that they've got away if I'm to be honest Sergeant,' said Jamie Riley. 'They would never have got a fair trial with Fitzsimons presiding.'

O'Keefe was nodding in agreement when the harbour clerk said, 'You can still catch up with them if you're quick, the ship will be in at Derry till tomorrow morning.'

Jamie Riley said, 'We're not going there, are we? It's about seventy or eighty miles away.'

'I think that we have to. If we don't and Fitzsimons finds out that the ship pulled in there our jobs could be at stake. Don't worry I'll drive for a while, and you can snooze in the carriage.'

The pair drove overnight and the next day to Derry taking turns at driving and sleeping and at a steady pace for the sake of the horse, stopping at intervals to let it rest and feed themselves and the horse, in the hope that the ship would have departed long before their arrival, little knowing that the ship was delayed for a further twenty-four hours.

Liam, Sarah, Hannah, and Connor emerged into the light together. The small amount of oxygen from the damaged cover and the fact that they had clung together near the ladder at the side of the hold had saved their lives. Many of the captives were lying together not moving. It was only when the hatch cover was removed, and oxygen levels restored that some who had been near death began to awaken.

Some other fortunate family groups who had also been incarcerated at the sides of the hold began to follow the Doyle's. Leaving many of the living below screaming and crying at the loss of their loved ones. The stench of the hold which had been dreadful before their deaths was now unbearable.

The captain was just beginning to wake up to his error of judgment and lack of humanity now ordered his crew to bring out the living into the fresh air.

It later became the task of the harbour master, the dock workers, and the local police to bring out the dead and begin the identification process.

Liam and Sarah looked in vain for their friends Finn and Robyn Kennedy among the living and were unable to find them. The dead were brought from the ship and placed on blankets in rows by the quayside. The problem of identifying the dead came next to the harbour master and his team. The living passengers were asked to help. Many could not be identified as they were travelling alone, or with false names or without any of the other passengers knowing them. Some could be named by their grieving families.

Liam asked his family to stay behind whilst he went forward to look for Finn and Robyn.

He could barely recognise them with their contorted blackened faces, but he was certain that it was them, they were yards apart from each other. Tears came to his eyes, and he could barely speak, 'These two people should lie together and be buried together.'

'Who are they?' said the harbour master's assistant.

Liam Doyle almost choked on his next words, first because of deep sorrow at the death of his two best friends and second because he was lying. 'They are Liam and Sarah Doyle. They had a son and daughter with them Hannah and Connor I haven't seen them among the survivors, and I can't identify them among all these poor young people the faces are too damaged.'

He returned to his family who immediately saw that he was in great stress. 'Have you found the Kennedy's?' asked Sarah.

'Yes, and I have done something dreadful to try and protect us now and, in the future, and I am ashamed of myself for doing it.'

'What have you done?'

'I have said that they are us, that we are dead to stop us from being chased and hounded in the future by the Fitzsimons family, for the rest of this voyage I am Finn Kennedy, you are Robyn and you two are Patrick and Eileen.'

O'Keeffe and Riley approached the dock at Kerry and to their dismay they found that the ship SS Londonderry was still at the quayside. They began to walk towards the dock. As they did so Constable Riley said, 'Can we think of a way out of this? I really don't want to take Liam and his family back to the mercy of the Fitzsimons brood.'

Connor and Hannah Doyle gathered around their parents trying to console them for the loss of their friends, and to placate Liam for what they considered to be his necessary deception.

Connor, with alarm in his voice, suddenly said, 'None of this matters we are about to be found out and taken back.'

They looked in the direction Connor was pointing and to their dismay saw Sergeant O'Keeffe and Constable Riley from Ballina walking towards the quayside where the bodies were laid.

The officers approached the clerk to whom Liam had spoken and they were taken to where the body of Robyn had just been placed next to Finn.

Liam said, 'Please stay here leave this with me.'

He approached the three men looking down at the body of Finn Kennedy and hear the clerk say, 'These are the bodies of

Liam and Sarah Doyle identified to me a few minutes ago by Mr Kennedy.'

The clerk looked up and said, 'Ah, here comes Mr Kennedy now.'

Liam walked towards them, his intention being to say that he was the man who struck Darrah Fitzsimons who was at the time attempting to rape his daughter.

Liam walked up to the three men and before he could speak, Sergeant O'Keeffe said, 'Hello Finn, nice to see you again. I didn't know you were leaving Ireland. I understand that you have already identified the body of Liam and Sarah Doyle. Unfortunately their kids are also dead.' He said looking towards the Doyle family standing a few yards away. He turned to the clerk and said, 'Yes, I can confirm Mr Kennedy's identification. Ah well that saves me the job of taking them back to Ballina to face the Fitzsimons family, come Mr Kennedy let me walk with you.'

Away from earshot he turned to Liam and spoke, 'Listen Liam neither you, nor your family must ever discuss what just happened or all our necks will be on the line.'

'Thank you, Mr O'Keeffe it will never be mentioned again after this day, I can assure you.'

'Go with God, Liam.'

At that the two officers walked away.

Chapter Eight

The remainder of the journey to Liverpool was cold, wet, and seemingly long with the surviving passengers doing their utmost to find whatever shelter was available and to stay out of the way of the scowling crew.

On the second day they arrived at the Albert Dock in the city, Liam and his family were surprised at the number of ships which were docked along the Quayside and the vast number of dock workers plying their back-breaking trade of removing goods from some ships from foreign ports and stacking goods in others for export abroad.

He explained to Connor and Hannah that Liverpool was the busiest port in the world outside London, and their biggest problem for the next few days was finding somewhere cheap to stay as their finances were quickly dwindling. Then finding work if they were to make enough money to travel onwards to their destination Canada or the United States of America.

They disembarked and stood with their meagre possessions in the quietest corner they could find in this teeming dockland wondering what on earth they had let themselves in for and what they were going to do next.

They need not have worried too much as thirty percent of the population of Liverpool at that time was made up of Irish people most of whom had been in similar situations themselves at some time.

Unknown to the family, they were being studied from across the quay by a small elderly woman.

The lady walked up to them as they were discussing their next move and spoke, 'Have you just arrived from Ireland,' in a pronounced Belfast accent.

'Yes,' replied Sarah.

'I am looking for a decent family. I have two rooms to let. I charge three shilling a week in advance if you are interested.'

'Yes, we are very interested,' said Sarah with deep relief in her voice.

'I am Sally Mullins. My house is about a ten-minute walk from here please follow me.'

They followed Sally through the dock gates and into the gloom of Liverpool's dock workers homeland. After a few minutes, they approached Drake Street. The houses were back-to-back terraces with twenty houses in the row, served by six outside toilets, three at either end of the row, the waste matter being taken away by an extension of the river Mersey part of which flowed under the toilet seats.

The street was so narrow and the houses opposite so close that even on this bright autumn morning, the sun was unable to penetrate adding to the gloominess of the surroundings.

Sally's house was near the middle of the row. There was a front door from the filthy narrow street and no back door. Two rooms upstairs and two rooms down.

Sally led them into the downstairs rooms which they found neat and tidy. There were gas cooking facilities, a coal fire and seating in one room and two double beds in the second with clean sheets. Gas lighting was available in both rooms.

Sally explained that she had left Belfast with her late husband Thomas ten years before. He had been a dock worker in Belfast, and they came to Liverpool for the slightly higher wages. They had enough money to buy the house on arrival, but Tom had died from Typhus five years ago. Since then she had been able to make a small living by renting the downstairs of the house and living herself in a self-contained flat upstairs.

'People come and go all the time. When a family leave, I go to the docks and try to find decent Irish people to rent my rooms, the problem is that they stay for a short while then move on. Please settle in and make yourselves comfortable. There are food shops just round the corner and a pub for the men. The toilets are at either end of the block. If you need anything, please let me know.'

'Thank you, Mrs Mullins.'

'Sally please.'

After she left, the family sat together and discussed their situation. They were aware that they did not yet have the funds to travel to North America, nor did they envisage staying in Liverpool for more than a short time, even though they had a reasonably comfortable billet. The city of Liverpool had a population of about three hundred and fifty thousand people, and they were unused to city dwelling.

'But we are here for now and we have to make a living. Let's just settle in for today and ask Sally's advice tomorrow.'

The next morning, they called Sally into their part of the house. Liam spoke, 'Sally, we have only got a quite small amount of money and we need to find employment to keep us going for the time being. Can you suggest anything?'

'What skills have you got?'

'I am a stone mason and Connor here is learning the trade.'

'Well, for you Liam I know that St Georges Hall on Lime Street has been under construction for a few years now and they are always on the lookout for stone masons, it's about a mile and a half from here. You might try going round there and speaking to the site manage.'

'What is St Georges Hall?'

'It's being built as a court and a centre for music. I am told that it will be magnificent when it is finished.' She looked at Connor.

'Connor, you are young, and fit can you stand really hard labour?'

'Yes.'

'Then why not try to get taken on as a lumper.'

'What on earth is a lumper?'

'It's an unskilled dock worker. They stand early every morning outside the gates at the Albert dock and wait to be taken on for the day. There are always more men than jobs, but a lot of the older ones are unfit drunks and wasters the bosses will only take them if there is no one else. If you like I will lend you Tom Stevedore's hook that will make you look the part and from then on, it's up to you.'

The next morning at seven saw young Connor Doyle standing, hook in hand, amongst about two hundred other men; young, middle aged and elderly. Some looking fit and eager, others stinking of the previous evening's booze, and yet others looking ill and careworn.

As the foremen approached to select the day's labourers Connor, the new boy, was suddenly and unexpectedly pushed violently to the rear by some of the more experienced men, surrounded and made invisible to the foremen.

Unexpected that is by Connor, but not to Charlie Simms one of the more observant foremen. The selection process began, and Connor became a little more exposed. The daily process only took a few minutes, and the gangs began to walk away to their day's work. Connor was one of half a dozen men not selected and came into full view.

'I want one more,' shouted Simms. You lad I've not seen you before. Where did you get that hook?'

'My landlady loaned it to me.'

'Who's your landlady?'

'Mrs Mullins.'

'I thought that I recognised Tom's old hook. What experience have you got?'

'I'm strong and hardworking, and willing to learn sir.'

Simms looked at one of the men he had hired. 'Jemmy, are you willing to take him on as your partner?'

Connor recognised Jemmy as one of the men who had tried to push him into obscurity.

Smiling Jemmy said, 'Aye I'll do that sir.'

'Teach him all you know, should take about five minutes.'

Liam, together with his bag of tools, walked the mile and a half to Lime Street and he found the building site for St Georges Hall. It was massive, larger by far than Liam had anticipated. Though the builders had been working the site for years it was far from complete. Maybe, Liam guessed no more than half built at that stage.

He approached the entrance to the site and spoke to the gate keeper who he discovered was also Irish. Liam explained why he was there, and the gatekeeper directed him towards some wooden shacks where he could speak with the site manager.

The manager Ivor Coulson after listening to Liam said, 'We are always on the lookout for decent stone masons. We'll give you a trial and if you are any good, we will take you on.'

They walked across to the stone mason's yard where Coulson spoke to a large middle-aged man who was cutting stone as they entered.

'Rufus. This is Liam Doyle just arrived from the Emerald Isle, check his credentials please, I'll be back in about an hour.'

Rufus Tetley, a large jovial Lancastrian from the coal mining town of Wigan, said, 'Ok Liam let's see how you shape up. See that stone that I am working on. That's will form part of the external cornice of the building eventually.' He pulled out a plan drawing. 'These are what we are looking to make. We will start of two stones together; you copy me, and we will see how we go.'

Liam slipped on his linen mask he wore whenever he worked with stone. He noted that Rufus did not wear anything on his face.

One hour later, Liam was keeping up with Rufus who could see that his work was at least as good as his own. 'Ok Liam, when Mr Coulson comes back, I will recommend that he employs you. He will offer you thirty shillings a week. Stick out for thirty-five that's what the rest of us are on. We don't yet have a union, but we do stick together and some of the lads might not want to work with you if you took less.'

Liam would have been delighted with thirty shillings and regular work, but he felt obliged to go along with Rufus.

In the event, thirty shillings was indeed offered by Coulson and Liam said that he would happily commence work the following morning but only if the offer was thirty-five shillings.

Coulson gave Tetley a withering look and with seemingly great reluctance agreed to Liam's demand.

As Coulson walked away, Rufus said, 'Well done Liam lad, at thirty-five bob a week you'll be welcomed into the team.'

'What do you mean thirty-five bobs?

'A bob means a shilling in Lancashire. Have you never heard the expression, oh two tanners, two tanners make a bob, three make one and six and four two bob?'

'What's a tanner in Lancastrian? I always thought that it was a man who cures leather.'

'Aye and it's also a sixpence.'

'Liam, nearly half the men working on this site are Irish. You'll get used to us and we'll all get along great.'

At lunchtime that day, Rufus took Liam to a large wooden hut which served as a canteen and the good, humoured banter continued.

After they had eaten Rufus stood up with some of his English colleagues and they chanted;

> Your Bob owes our Bob a bob and if your Bob don't
> Give our Bob that bob as your Bob owes our Bob
> Our Bob will give your Bob a bob on't nose.

The Irish in the canteen laughed. They stood up as group, dragging Liam with them and sang.

> Oh the Scousers came and tried to teach us their ways.
> They scorned us for being what we are.
> But they might as well go try and catch a moonbeam.
> Or light a penny candle from a star.

It became clear to Liam that he would enjoy working with this group of people who could show respect and pull each other's legs at the same time.

Over on the docks, Connor was learning that being a lumper was not simply a matter of pulling and pushing. There was a high level of skill to be learnt. Jemmy was teaching him how to assess the size and weight of the objects being loaded or unloaded, otherwise the carts taking goods away could become top heavy and collapse. The ships' captains would not be happy if the loaded weight was one sided and the ship listed as it drew out of the harbour. Jemmy Hartley and Connor soon became confirmed friends.

Hydraulic cranes were being tested by other crews, but Charlie Simms' crew were working the old-fashioned way, loading and unloading with hooks, ropes chains and ramps, testing Connor's strength and stamina to the utmost. He was beginning to feel muscles he never knew existed and for most of his first week he was in constant agony.

The weeks went by, and Liam and Connor were working hard, earing good money and relatively happy with their new life. Things were not quite so good for Sarah and Hannah. Satisfying work was not easy to find in the city for women and whilst their living conditions and food supplies were comfortable, both longed for quieter country conditions away from the city and the chance to find suitable employment.

Chapter Nine

It was the beginning of March 1849 and Darrah Fitzsimons was almost fully recovered from his injury and resuming his hedonistic lifestyle. It had irked him for some time that whenever he visited the Gill's farm the three females had almost always recently gone shopping, and he so much enjoyed tormenting them by touching and brushing against them in the more intimate areas of their bodies.

On his most recent visit, they were again missing. He asked one of the farm hands if there was a second entrance and exit to the farm and was told that there was a small back gate one hundred yards further along the lane leading to the local village.

He sent word that he would attend the farm at ten the next morning to inspect the book records.

At a few minutes to ten, he was astride his horse behind a bush near the small gate when he saw the donkey and small cart heading his way with the three females aboard. As they approached, he jumped from the horse and stood in their way.

'Good morning, ladies. I hope that you are not going anywhere I want you in your kitchen making my lunch. In fact I insist that you turn back to do so.'

'Sorry Mister Fitzsimons we are just going shopping, we will be back in about one hour.'

'I think not ladies. I insist you turn back now or suffer the consequences.'

'Knowing that she had no other choice Emily Gill began to turn the cart back towards the farm.'

'Wait a minute.' Fitzsimons shouted. 'I've seen that donkey and cart before, I'm sure. Stop where you are.'

He approached the cart and looked at the wooden side. 'See that strut there. I broke that with my fist months ago. That donkey and cart belonged to Sarah, and Hannah Doyle. You must have bought it from them.'

'No, my husband bought it from a man called Finn Kennedy who was on his way to Sligo some months ago.'

'When?'

Emily had no time to think and spoke, 'December.'

Fitzsimons was a nasty man, but he was not totally stupid. 'Finn Kennedy disappeared from my farm at the same time as the Doyle family, travelling towards Sligo. They caught the same ship and Doyle and his family died. They must have been together when you bought this.'

'I'm sure that they weren't Mister Fitzsimons.'

'And I am certain that they were. This has just cost you your farm.' He laughed. 'Tell Gill to get packing, you'll get your notice tomorrow.'

Fitzsimons rode off down the lane laughing and delighted with himself. He had not failed to notice how beautiful the elder daughter Emelia was and imagined himself with her as he rode home.

On reporting the meeting to her husband, Emily was devastated and blaming herself. John Gill said, 'No love. I was stupid enough to buy the rig in the first place. I've hated working for that family for years. We have money tucked away. Don't worry we'll get by whatever happens.'

They discussed the matter further that evening and decided that the Fitzsimons family would now make it impossible for them to find further similar employment in Ireland. 'We are still in our thirties,' said John. 'Let's move on like so many Irish families are doing. Let us make our way to Liverpool. Then take a ship to Canada for a new life.'

They packed that evening in anticipation. Then the following morning they called in the farm hands as they came to work and told them that they were leaving later that day for Sligo, their intention being to travel to Liverpool then on to Canada.

Mid-morning that same day, Fitzsimons arrived with one of his cronies in his father's carriage. With obvious delight he served the notice to quit upon John Gill and spoke, 'This is my friend Michael McCarthy, he will be taking your place as manager of this farm. I want you and yours gone from here by lunchtime today.'

'Will be gone on our way to Sligo, and we are happy to go within the hour.' He smiled in the face of his adversary and spoke, 'Canada, here we come.'

Fitzsimons, who was angered by Gill's obvious joy at leaving the farm, saw that Emily and her daughters were loading the small donkey cart ready to go.

'You can't take that cart with you it belongs to the farm.'

'Indeed not sir. I bought this with my own money. It's mine and we are leaving with it.'

Gill went into the farmhouse to collect the last of their belongings. Fitzsimons called McCarthy to him and spoke,

'Come on, you can start here later. We have work to do.' They abruptly left heading towards Sligo.

Fitzsimons malevolent mind was working overtime during the journey. He was determined to make life as difficult and miserable for the Gill's as possible.

On arrival at the docks, he assumed a sympathetic and endearing facial expression, the one he had practiced many times on his schoolteachers, his father and mother when he wanted something he was not supposed to have.

First, he approached a group of teenaged girls who were dancing and entertaining travellers to earn a few pennies.

He and McCarthy began the rumour that the Gill family who would soon be at the quayside to board the outgoing steamship they had systematically bullied, assaulted in every possible way, enslaved, and abused their eldest daughter, Emelia. They were trying to smuggle her out of the country before she complained about them to the authorities. He was attempting to rescue her from their tyranny and return her to her favourite aunt whom she loved dearly and who would take care of her.

He described Emelia and the donkey and cart they would come in.

To Fitzsimons' delight, the girls spread the rumour very quickly throughout the dockyard. People, including dock workers, began to carefully watch all families approaching the docks.

On their way to the docks, John Gill explained to his family that they may be a little late for a ship that day. 'No matter we can stay at one of the boarding houses for a ship later in the week.'

They arrived and were unaware of the hostile looks they were receiving from others at the quayside. The ship was taking on the last few passengers. Gill saw the dancing girls coming towards him. 'Girls, if I give you this donkey and cart for your own use will you take care of them?'

'Of course, we will Mister Gill.'

They grabbed their baggage and made towards the ramp. A thought flashed through his brain. *How do they know my name?*

The thought vanished as he saw that the gate to the ramp was about to close.

They moved forward quickly and heard the steward shout. 'Right you're the last ones. They moved through and the gate slammed behind them.

As they arrived at the top of the ramp, it was immediately pulled away and the family stopped to catch their breath. The anchoring ropes below were being cast off and the ship began to move.

Emily screamed. 'Where's Emelia?'

'She couldn't have gone far; she has to be here,' shouted John Gill.

As he looked over the ship's rail onto the quayside, he saw his eldest daughter shouting and crying among the teenage dancers, being dragged towards a carriage and an evil, smiling Darrah Fitzsimons who looked up at Gill and waved and dragged Emelia into his carriage.

John Gill was in total despair. He, at first, wanted to leap over the ship's side to attempt to retrieve his daughter. He knew that was impracticable as he could not swim and, in any case, he had to protect the rest of his family.

He went to the ship's bridge shouting for the captain to return to shore. The captain completely ignored him.

One of the crew shouted, 'Whatever it is, forget it. He won't turn the ship around for any reason.'

The Gill family then faced a two-day journey to Liverpool. Something they had looked forward to with great pleasure, the start of a new life together, now in complete devastation. Several times during the voyage it crossed John Gill's mind that if his daughter had died, at least she would be at peace. As it was, she was in the hands of a brute who would abuse and humiliate her. He made his mind up that on arrival in Liverpool, he would find his family accommodation then return on the next ship to rescue Emelia.

Chapter Ten

The trip seemed interminable, but eventually the Gill family arrived at their destination and walked down the ramp into the Albert dock. As they walked across the dockyard towards the exit a gang of dock workers were standing by to begin to unload the ship's cargo.

A voice from the gang resounded in John Gills ears. 'Mister Gill, Emily, what are you doing here?'

A young man walked from the gang towards them. Emily Gill almost fainted as she saw the ghost. John Gill shouted, 'Connor Doyle. We thought you were dead.'

'It's just a rumour,' Connor Doyle said flippantly. He looked around and spoke, 'Where's Emelia?'

At that remark, the whole family broke down. At first Connor could not understand what they were saying, and eventually when he did his old feelings of love for Emelia Gill returned and he also broke down sobbing.

Moments later the foreman Simms saw the emotional group, although he did not understand what was happening, he was a fair and understanding man. 'Whatever it is Connor, you had better take the rest of this shift off so that you can sort things out. I'll hire somebody in your place.'

Connor took the Gill family to his home where they found Sarah and Hannah and the natural emotions again built to a high level so much that Mrs Mullins came downstairs to investigate.

When things calmed a little, John Gill said, 'I am catching the steamer back to Sligo tomorrow and I will confront Fitzsimmons at the manor and give him the hell he deserves.'

Connor spoke up, 'Mister Gill. You must stay here with your family, it makes sense. Fitzsimons will be expecting you and will have nasty reception waiting for you, he won't be expecting me. Your family needs you now and will need you even more in the future. If anything happens to you, they will suffer. I will go back to Ireland tomorrow. I will find Emelia and bring her back to you.'

Emily Gill said, 'John, you know that he is right, please stay here with us, we need you!'

Reluctantly and after much persuasion, John Gill agreed.

Mrs Mullins chipped in, 'John and Emily. I know a nice lady two streets from here who has rooms free now, I'll take you round there when you are ready.'

Later that day when Liam arrived home from work, he was unhappy that his son should be putting himself in such great danger, but eventually and for the same family reasons which had persuaded John Gill, he allowed his son to go.

The following morning the eighteen-year-old Connor, whom life and circumstances had aged physically and mentally beyond his years, with money and a pack full of food became a passenger on the returning steam ship to Sligo.

Two days later, he left the ship and began the long trudge to Stokane, and the farm recently vacated by John Gill and family as his first port of call.

It was not yet daylight and as he walked from the town, he heard a pony and cart pulling up the hill behind him. He turned, hoping that the driver would be kind enough to offer a lift. The driver was about to drive straight ahead when he looked at Connor and shouted, 'Are you Connor Doyle or are you a ghost. We all thought that you were dead.'

Connor recognised the driver as Cillian McMahon a classmate from his old schooldays. 'Nah, it was just a rumour,' he reiterated, a joke he had begun to enjoy. 'Are you going to give this spectre a lift or what?'

'What?' shouted McMahon also enjoying the moment.

As they sat together aboard the cart, Cillian began to question Connor. 'You got a job as a dock worker in Liverpool. Why have you returned?'

Connor was reluctant to tell Cillian the reason and spoke, 'Just some family matters to sort out then I'll be going back, listen I need two favours first, please don't tell anyone that you have seen me and second, I want to drop off briefly at John Gill's old place in Stokane, will you wait on the road for me?'

'Sure.'

Half an hour's ride from Sligo, they came to a wooded area with dark trees on both sides of the road, it was gloomy, not quite daylight when they entered the wood. Suddenly a man appeared in front of them pointing an old army musket at them and ordered them to stop. Connor recognised the man immediately. He was Joseph O'Neil, one of the two Fitzsimons family gamekeepers, who had chased Connor and other children years before when they were trespassing. They were in fear of him and knew that if he caught them, they were in for a severe beating. He was ex-army, tough and known to be capable of anything including murder.

He looked them up and down, did not recognise the now grown-up Connor. Checked the cart which was empty. A voice from the woods shouted, 'Is he there?'

'No, just two snot nosed kids.'

O'Neil inclined his head south, indication that they were free to go, which they did very quickly.

'What the hell was that about?' said Cillian as they drove off.

'No idea,' lied Connor, knowing full well that had Gill been with them O'Neil would be burying him, including any witnesses in the woods about now.

They arrived near the farm. It was early morning and some of the farm hands would, Connor was aware be in the cow shed for the early morning milking. He wanted to speak with Thomas Rafferty, a man he trusted and had got to know well during the wall building. He did not want to be seen by Michael McCarthy, the new manager.

He spotted Rafferty in the far corner on a stool among all the other milk men and maids and cautiously approached. 'My God young Doyle, I thought you were dead.'

Connor avoided his usual comment. 'No I'm very much alive Mister Rafferty. Is McCarthy about?'

'Heaven no. We rarely see him till lunchtime. It's good to see you Connor, are you here to stay?'

'No. Have you heard that Fitzsimons kidnapped Emelia Gill before she was able to board the ship at Sligo?'

'We all heard a rumour, but we all thought that was a crime too far, even for him.'

'Well it's true and I am looking for her. And I wondered he had hidden her here.'

Thomas Rafferty was astounded at the news. 'No, definitely not. We haven't seen Darrah Fitzsimons since the Gill's, bless them, left here. He was only interested in Emily and her daughters.'

'Please don't tell McCarthy that I have been here.'

'Don't worry on that score young Connor, he's a waste of space. This place will go to the dogs unless he is replaced soon. Good luck finding Emelia. If there's anything I can do, let me know.'

Cillian had been as good as his word and was waiting for Connor. As they progressed towards Ballina. Now that the rabbit was out of the bag, he decided that he might as well tell Cillian the real reason for his return. Cillian was astonished, but practical. 'I think that you should see Sergeant O'Keeffe and seek his help.'

'I need to try myself first. I promise that I will ask for his help if I don't find her today, please keep this quiet for now.'

The pair rode on towards Ballina, as they approached the old Kennedy farm.

Connor asked Cillian to stop for a moment. He banged on the door, there was no reply, he tried the door handle it was unlocked so he went inside. There was no sign of Emelia.

'Will you drop me at our old cottage?' he asked Cillian. 'I need somewhere to stay while I search for her.'

'I think that you will find that Fitzsimons has possessed your old place after you left. I don't think anyone lives there.'

The remark gave Connor food for thought. 'Drop me there anyway. I'll check the old place out.'

As he dropped Conner off, Cillian said, 'Let me know how you go on; you know where I live.'

Connor walked down the familiar path to his old cottage. He stopped at the door and saw that it was fitted with a large padlock and hasp. He banged on the door. There was no reply. He was about to walk away when something, some instinct he could not later describe told him to enter the cottage the old way through the faulty window and check the place over, even if the feeling he got was just nostalgia.

He climbed into his old bedroom and walked through into the old living quarters. The smell was dreadful and there he saw a sight that would live with him for the rest of his life.

Lying on the old rug in front of the fireplace what his first petrified thought assumed was the dead body of Emelia Gill. Her face was bruised, and she lay naked and still, thin, and ashen. Her hair matted with bile, and her lower body encrusted with dried excrement. Bound with her hands behind her back and her feet forced up behind her body and tied within an inch of her hands. Her body was also bruised and felt cold to his touch. There were fresh splashes of dried blood near the body. He was certain that she had died in agony.

Connor collapsed in the corner of the room and cried like he had not done so even as a child, he had lost his love, the one he had travelled many miles for, the one he would happily die for himself.

He eventually pulled himself together; he wished to see to her dignified even in death. He got up and found his mother's rabbit skinning knife and cut away the ropes binding her. He laid her on clean blankets and covered her with sheets. It was cold in the cottage, so he found kindling and lit the peat fire.

Connor then went outside to fetch water which he heated on the fire and began to wash Emelia.

As he did so he thought that he felt a slight movement, a small shiver under his hand. 'Wishful thinking,' he muttered. But there it was again, hardly anything at all, but it gave him something, a smattering of hope. He remembered when he was a child, he had seen the doctor hold a glass jar at the mouth and nose of his grandfather before pronouncing him dead. He found one of his mother's glass jars and held it to her nose. He saw a tiny spot of steam gather on the glass.

'She's alive,' he shouted and began to rub vigorously at the deep welts on her wrists and ankles caused by the rope. He saw clearly that her hands and feet which had been a purple colour was beginning to return to normal. He was greatly encouraged; he felt her shoulders and they seemed to be warming. He wrapped her in the sheets and drew her closer to the fire. He lay on the floor beside her and held her close, face to face, to share his body heat. After a short while, he could feel some movement and he heard her moan.

Suddenly, an hour or so later she opened her eyes, looked at him smiled and spoke, 'Connor are we in heaven.' She closed her eyes immediately and fell into a deep untroubled sleep.

Connor went into the bedroom and brought a straw mattress which he placed before the fire. He laid her on it with her head on a pillow, he covered her with sheets and a blanket. Then he sat and watched her sleeping and breathing normally. She had recognised him, and he was completely transformed from the Connor of an hour before. He was now the happiest he had ever been and was content to simply watch her until she awakened when he would make sure she was fed and had something to drink.

Two hours later, she opened her eyes and gave Connor a slightly startled and confused look and the words tumbled out of her mouth, 'Are we alive, where are we? I thought that you were dead and there you are. I don't understand.'

'Yes Emelia. We are very much alive; we are in our old family cottage near Ballina. You have been abused by Darrah Fitzsimons. I did not die on the ship, and I am now here to look after you. You will never be abused by anyone again.'

She began to weep. 'I never thought that I would see you again. I am so happy.'

Connor helped her to sit up and placed a cushion behind her back against the wall.

'Are you hungry?'

'I don't think that I have eaten for days.'

He picked up his food pack and mixed bread and biscuit crumbs together in warm water into a soup and gently fed her from a spoon. He knew not to give her too much at once following her ordeal and gave her water which he had previously boiled.

'How long have I been here?'

'It's six days since he snatched you from your family.'

She began to reminisce. 'I was with my sisters about to get on the ship when a group of dancing girls surrounded me and started to pull me away. I shouted that I wanted to get on the ship and one of them kept saying that she knew that I was being abused by my father and they were helping me to get to my aunt. I could not escape from them, and they pushed me into Fitzsimons's carriage where I was held by a man I did not know. The ship left without me and Darrah Fitzsimons started to say things like: "Don't worry my love I will take good care of you; your dad has left you in my charge."

Tears were rolling down her cheeks and Connor said, 'Please stop, this is upsetting you too much.'

'No I want to get this off my mind. I want to tell you then you will understand that I did not leave my family deliberately.'

'No one ever thought that of you.'

'He brought me here and for the first three days he had me manacled to the iron bedrail. He fed me and tried to soft talk me into being his voluntary mistress. I told him in no uncertain terms where to go. On the fourth day, he began to lose his temper and he hit me a few times and told me that I was a stupid woman, he was rich and would make me wealthy and comfortable if I would please him. I told him that I would never do that, and he really beat me. He gave me no food or water that day. He manacled me that night away from the bed where I could get no comfort and was very cold.'

'Please stop now, this is so hard for me to hear.'

'No I must finish then you know it all.'

'Where he left me, I found some iron knitting needles on that shelf behind you. I took one and rubbed it against the stone floor until the point was sharp.'

'Yes, my mother always kept those on that shelf.'

He came on the fifth day, which must have been yesterday and completely lost his mind. He ripped my clothes off until I was naked. Then he took his own clothes off and I saw that he was roused. He was about to rape me. He came at me, and I had the needle in my right hand. I stabbed with it, and it went right through his groin, you know what I mean and into his lower belly, I pulled it back out and threw it down. He was then bleeding, obviously in pain and raging at me, he tied me up the way you found me and as he went through the door, he shouted something like, 'Die in agony bitch.'

Ah, thought Connor, *that explains the blood marks on the floor.*

'I was in agony and could hardly breathe. I think that I lost consciousness and I was dreaming of you, when I woke and saw you, I knew you were dead, and I thought that I was in heaven.'

There was, for a short time, a heavy yet comfortable silence between them as Connor tried to imagine the trauma Emelia had endured at the hands of a brute, and the amount of bravery she had shown in not succumbing to his will. Emelia looked upon Connor as her knight errant, her saviour and gallant rescuer. The love between them which had been there before blossomed.

He helped her to dress in her old torn clothing.

'How are your hands and feet now?' he asked.

'The pain is subsiding and the feeling in my hands has returned.'

'Can you try to stand and walk?'

'I'll try.'

With his help she stood and as she began to walk around the room the pain returned to her feet as the blood circulation improved. She perceived with effort and the pain eventually subsided.

He fed her more gruel this time adding a little smoked ham from his pack, and she began to feel more normal, the feeling had returned to both her hands and feet. Her youth and general fitness had prevailed, and she had quickly made a full physical recovery. The mental scars would take a little longer.

'I think that we should sleep here tonight, then, if you are up to it, we will begin to make our way towards Sligo tomorrow morning. Are you happy with that?'

'Yes, but what if he comes back?'

'Where is the sharp needle?'

'She handed it to him. 'I'll deal with him if he comes back tonight.'

They heard the heavy rain outside. Darkness came about seven and they were happily chatting about the future when they both heard a sound which they had dreaded, the padlock on the door being unlocked.

'Go into the bedroom and leave him to me.'

'No, we're in this together,' she replied.

Fitzsimons came through the door; he was soaking wet from the rainfall, and he expected to find a cold house and a corpse to get rid of. Instead he walked into a warm room and two very healthy young people. He stared and his face briefly drained of colour. 'Connor Doyle. You're supposed to be dead.'

Connor couldn't help himself. 'Just a rumour, you shouldn't take them seriously.'

'It won't be a rumour in a few minutes it will be true, you'll both be dead meat,' shouted Fitzsimons remembering the last time they had a confrontation and how easily he had thrown Connor from this same house, but this time he was taking no chances. He pulled a pistol from his belt. He had intended to shoot Emelia if she had still been alive, now it came in much more useful. He immediately pointed the pistol at Connor and pulled the trigger. Connor froze, expecting to die, the pistol was single shot, old army weapon he had taken from his father's collection. He had used it before successfully and primed and loaded it himself. He had never shot at anything that was likely to shoot back and he was unaware of the adage 'Keep your powder dry.' The pistol was not happy with wet primer and powder, there was just a click, then nothing.

He laughed. 'No problem, now it's a club to beat you with.' What he did not know was that Connor had been a lumper at Liverpool docks for more than three months since their last encounter, he was smaller and lighter than his opponent but was now at least as strong and much fitter.

Ignoring Emelia completely, he came towards Connor wielding the pistol like a club and aimed for Connor's head. He ducked and grabbed Fitzsimons by both wrists pushing him backwards across the room. Emelia saw what was happening and she dodged behind them and dropped to her hands and knees on the floor. Connor propelled Fitzsimons towards her and as they got near, he pushed with all his might. Darrah Fitzsimons tripped and fell heavily onto the hard stone floor. They both heard the crack as his head hit the ground. His fractured skull, not yet fully recovered from his previous injury was burst wide open and he died instantly.

Connor and Emelia were mortified. All they had planned to do was escape the clutches of this evil man and now they had killed him. 'What do we do now?' she said.

They sat in dazed silence for about an hour, until Connor looked through the now unlocked door and spoke, 'I want you to stay here for the time being and get some rest. I need to get rid of the body. If he is found here his father will have the world come down on us. No one in authority will believe that he had kidnapped you and was trying to kill us both. His horse is outside, and I will take him away.'

'What will you do with him?'

'I'm going to take him to the lake. If Shamus Teal's boat is where he usually keeps it, I will weight him and sink him in the middle, please stay here, this is my job.'

After a while she agreed that if they were to travel the next day she needed to rest. 'Be careful,' she said.

'Shall I lock the door while I am gone?'

'No I don't ever want to be locked in anywhere again ever.'

Between them they completed the disagreeable task of draping the body on the back of the horse and Connor led the horse away. It was now late evening, completely dark with the moon shrouded by cloud and Connor felt relatively safe with his burden. He was wrong to feel that way.

Even in the darkness he was familiar with the terrain and had no problem finding the way. He entered the wooded area just before the lake and walked along the path between the trees, unexpectedly the clouds cleared away and the moon shone brightly. He was still unconcerned, there was not likely to be anyone around the lake side at this time of day. He heard a voice from the woods and suddenly a dark figure burst out of the trees on his left and disappeared just as quickly into the trees on his right. Just as suddenly and without any warning, a second figure appeared from the trees. Panting and sweating Constable Riley stopped and was just as startled as Connor to be confronted by the ghost of Connor Doyle. 'You should not be here you are supposed to be dead, what are you doing here and what on earth is that?' he said pointing at the load.

'My god. Darrah Fitzsimons,' he shouted as he spotted the face. He blew his whistle to summon help and spoke, 'Connor Doyle what have you done?'

Puffing, panting, and wiping the sweat from his face, Sergeant O'Keeffe emerged from the trees. 'Oh I thought you had caught the poacher.' He too looked astounded to see Connor and his load.

'I think that explanations are demanded here, talk and talk fast, what is going on? Have you killed the swine and if you have why have you killed him?'

Connor, who could now see the hangman's noose dangling before him, told the whole story from the kidnapping to Fitzsimons's attempt to kill both himself and Emelia.

O'Keeffe and Riley were aghast, they had no idea until that moment that Emelia Gill was anywhere other than with her mother and father. 'All this was going on in our backyard without us knowing,' said O'Keeffe.

'He was a very deep, evil and devious man!' exclaimed Riley in their defence.

'Now I will tell you something Connor Doyle,' said O'Keeffe. 'His father Sean Fitzsimons died suddenly two weeks ago. He was in previous good health and Doctor Malone thinks that he was poisoned. We can't prove it, but it is our belief that the thing you have on the back of that horse poisoned his own father to take over the estate. I know that Sean has a brother living in London who will no doubt take over now. I don't know what he is like, we can only hope for the best. Where is Emelia Gill now?'

'At our old cottage.'

'What do you intend to do with that?' He was nodding towards the body.

'Use Shamus's boat and weight it down in the Conn.'

'Ah. Fish food, all that he was ever fit for, make a good job of it we don't ever want him to float. By the way, we never saw you here. When you return don't go back to your old cottage, we are going to get Emelia and take her to my house where she can be properly looked after by my wife.'

At that the pair swiftly disappeared into the woods whence they came, and the shadow of the noose crumbled before Connor's eyes, and he went on his way with a blithe spirit to do the local population a great favour and feed the fish in Lough Conn.

After completing his task, he returned to the home of Sergeant O'Keeffe with some trepidation unaware of how Emelia would take to the house move. He need not have worried he found her in fine fettle having a supper before being taken upstairs to bed by Mrs O'Keeffe. He was welcomed and given a supper before being shown to his not so sumptuous quarters, a wooden hut with a straw mattress and blanket behind the house, with the now well-fed and watered horse as a sleeping partner.

The following morning, Mrs O'Keeffe insisted that Emelia stayed with her for one more day. 'She must be fully recovered before travelling so far,' she said.

Connor was invited into the house for breakfast, and he saw that Emelia was looking wonderful with clean clothing donated by Mrs O'Keeffe and a glowing smiling face. Connor was delighted. During that day he found himself things to do looking after the horse and the sergeants back garden.

Later that day, Sergeant O'Keeffe found him grooming the horse in his back garden. 'Cillian is driving a load to Sligo tomorrow morning to meet a ship and I have arranged for yourself and Emelia to accompany him.'

'Thank you for everything. What about the horse I have grown rather fond of him?'

O'Keeffe laughed and spoke, 'You can't steal the horse on top of everything else. Don't worry about him I will return him to his stable tomorrow.'

Early the following morning and a lovely late March day, Cillian McMahon pulled up his horse and cart outside the house and Connor and Emelia were given a food pack for the journey, they profusely thanked Mr O'Keefe, a tearful Mrs O'Keeffe, and Constable Riley for all their help and they got on their way to Sligo.

The journey to Liverpool seemed very long to them but it was uneventful and two days later a bright early April Wednesday morning, they landed at the Albert dock.

Chapter Eleven

For six days since Connor's departure, the families Doyle and Gill have been in deep pain not knowing the fate of a daughter and a son. On day five, they had hopefully gathered at the dock to be desperately disappointed when no steamship had arrived there from Sligo. They were informed that a ship was due midmorning the next day.

From eight that Wednesday morning the whole of the two families had gathered at the dockside. Liam had taken the morning off and he was approached by Charlie Simms, one of the dock foremen. 'Your Connor Doyle's dad, aren't you?'

'Yes, we are hoping that he will arrive today with Emelia Gill.'

'Well I can tell you that the ship from Sligo is due in about ten this morning and I am with you. I've grown fond of Connor, he's one of my best workers and I hope that he is on it and has achieved what he set out to do.'

'Thank you.' He informed the families and they got together and said a prayer for the safe homecoming of their respective son and daughter.

The ship was late, at ten thirty Charlie Simms approached the families and spoke, 'That's it now coming into dock.'

As it came in, they all strained their eyes looking at the passengers lining the ships rail. Hannah Doyle had the keenest sight and shouted, 'I can see Connor look about the middle of the passengers.' She had never met Emelia and shouted, 'There is a girl standing alongside of him.'

Eileen Gill shouted excitedly, 'Yes, it's Emelia, I can see her clearly. They are both here.'

At that the two families were delirious with joy. Jumping up and down with excitement and tears rolling freely down faces, including the tough and weather-beaten faces of John Gill and Liam Doyle.

When they alighted from the ramp they were surrounded by their madly excited families, which for the moment included Charlie Simms and some of the dock workers who had become Connor's friends and were aware of his mission. Emelia was embraced by her loving family and Connor was carried shoulder high by the workers as they left the docks.

At the gate Simms put on his stern face, regained control and spoke, 'Right, back to work lads. Connor, be here at eight tomorrow, you've been off work for long enough, you'll be getting soft if we're not careful.'

That evening, they had a celebratory meal with beer and wine and began to discuss the future. It had been the Gill's family's intention to move on to America or Canada from Liverpool, but Connor and Emelia made it very clear that they were in love and could not see a future without each other. The guarded and unspoken question on the minds of the joint families was, 'Had she been raped whilst a prisoner of Fitzsimons, could she be pregnant with his baby?'

Emelia who had been waiting for the question, precipitated it by saying, 'I know that you are too considerate and kind to ask, but no Darrah Fitzsimons did not physically rape me, he tried hard to seduce me and eventually attempted to rape me, but I persuaded him otherwise with the help of one of Sarah's sharpened iron knitting needles. He had a fall and cracked his head, and he is now feasting with the devil and will not trouble us again.'

There was an audible sigh of relief.

Liam said that it had always been his intention eventually to move to the Americas when they could afford to travel in reasonable style, he did not wish to subject his family ever again to the dreadful indignity of steerage travel. It was his opinion that two years of work and saving money would allow them to travel in some comfort, with money to use once they arrived.

John made it clear that he wished to go to the land of the free at some time. He was happy to remain in England for now and for his daughter to marry Connor after a reasonable courtship. 'After what we have been through and all that Connor has done for us, I see us now as a united family and it would wonderful if we could stay together. But I am a farmer and I need work which I will not find in Liverpool.'

The ladies, particularly Sarah and Hannah did not wish to spend the next two years in Liverpool. 'We are country girls at heart and don't belong in the city, I also need work and I don't see myself as Maggie May cruising in Canning Place,' said Sarah to the amusement of the assembly.

It was agreed that they would all spend a week or so considering their options before a final decision was made.

At lunchtime the next day, Liam was mulling over the problem when Rufus came to his bench and sat with him. 'You look like you've got the world on your shoulders, you've got your lad back with his lass, you should be happy,' he said.

Rufus had become a good friend and Liam nodded and agreed that he was very happy to have his son and future daughter-in-law back and explained his new food for thought including the dilemma of the Gill family.

'Do you know?' said Rufus. 'I have been thinking of moving back towards Wigan. My mother getting on in age and is not well and I want to spend a bit more time with her. I have heard on the grapevine that Liverpool Corporation are looking for workers, well navvies and stone masons. They are building three reservoirs at a place called Rivington. It's in the Lancashire countryside just north of Wigan, there's at least a couple of year work lined up, the area might just suit your mate John Gill. They are recruiting in the Town Hall on Saturday morning. How about you, me and your lad Connor going along and see what happens.'

'Sounds great, let us try our luck.'

Without raising the hopes of the ladies, the three men attended Liverpool town hall at nine on the Saturday morning and waited in a small queue with others. At ten Rufus's name was called and he went forward into the interview room, Liam and Connor heard laughter as he entered and a short time later, they were called forward. 'This is Jack Grimes, he's a stone mason. We worked together years ago, he knows my work and I've got the job. I have recommended you two, but he wants to see your work before he can hire you.'

They went into the rear yard which was set up for the test. Liam passed with flying colours, but Connor showed promise but was less skilled.

'Ok,' said Grimes. Liam, 'we will take you on as a full-fledged stonemason. Connor, we will take you on as an improver to do the less skilled work. Your pay won't be as much.'

'How much will we be paid?' asked Rufus.

'What are you on now?' said Grimes.

'Forty shillings a week,' lied Rufus, with Liam nodding to back up the lie.

'Ok. Forty shillings for you two and thirty for Connor.'

A short time later when it came to signing the employment forms the three struggled to contain their excitement at their pay increase, when Grimes spoiled their fun a little by smiling at their obvious fibs. He knew the pay rates at St Georges Hall, and he announced that forty shillings a week was the going rate for the skilled work and long hours expected of them in any case. Their skills were badly needed at the site, and he had hoped that they would not demand more. *This way*, he mused, *everyone wins.*

'Ok,' said Grimes. 'Give your employers one week's notice and travel next Monday. I can issue you with railway warrants for you and your families. You will travel from Liverpool Great Howard Street railway station to Adlington Lancashire. It's a short walk from there to the site. How many do you need?'

Liam looked at Rufus who said, 'I know the way from there. Just one for me.'

'Ten please,' said Liam. 'We have a large family.'

Grimes blanched slightly but made out the warrant for ten.

As they left the Town Hall, Rufus said, 'Liam, do you mind if I come back with you. When you break the news, I would like to have a chat with the Gill family.'

That afternoon at Liam's request both families, together with Rufus, gathered in the Doyle's parlour. Liam and Connor broke the news that they were moving out the next Monday into the country and there was general excitement and delight among the Doyle's. 'I'm not sure what our accommodation with be like,' broached Liam. 'I feel sure that it will be pretty basic.'

'I can give you an idea,' said Rufus. 'It will probably be a wooden shack with beds with straw mattresses and a coal fired stove.'

'It will be whatever we make it and I'm sure we will be fine,' interjected Sarah.

The Gill family were looking a little apprehensive wondering what their part was in all this when Rufus spoke up.

'John, Emily and young ladies. I have a sister who is a farmer's wife. Their farm is just outside a town called Blackrod, north of Wigan and just across the valley from where me, and Liam's family will be living. It's a dairy farm, which I know you are familiar with, and they are always on the lookout for farm hands and milkmaids. They have a small cottage on their land. It's a bit run down and basic, but I am sure that you can make it comfortable. Bill and Nora, my brother-in-law and sister will probably work you quite hard. But they really are decent folk. When we arrive in the area, I will take you to them and introduce you. Then it's up to you.'

The pleasure on the faces of the Gill family told its own story.

'Right,' declared Liam. He went outside and brought in the packs of food and drinks they had collected on their way from the Town Hall. 'It's time to celebrate.' They went on to enjoy a splendid afternoon in each other's company. Rufus almost being accepted as a family member.

The next week went quickly by, the ladies went shopping and of course bought new clothing. Mrs Mullins was sorry to be losing her tenants whom she had found considerate, clean, and tidy. However she said that she would be at the docks on Monday looking for their replacement. Liam and Rufus gave notice of leaving their employment. Strictly speaking Connor had no reason to give notice, he had simply to fail to turn up, but he felt obliged to tell Charlie Simms that he was leaving. Charlie who had grown fond of Connor wished him all the luck in the world.

Early that Monday the families and Rufus, full of hope for the future, caught the train from Great Howard Street railway station, travelling through the lush mid-April Lancashire sunshine, arriving at Adlington railway station on the appropriately named Railway Road in the late morning. They had seen two rather well-dressed gentlemen sitting near them on the train as they spoke with some excitement about their new venture.

Rufus was taking the Gill's to his sister's farm, and he gave the Doyle's directions to the site. They had noticed a carriage and horses waiting at the station and other than admiring the horses thought no more of it. They set off walking up Railway Road when the carriage pulled up alongside and a rather well-spoken voice said, 'I could not help overhearing you on the train. You are going to the site of the reservoirs I understand.'

'Yes.'

'It would be remiss of me not to offer the ladies transport and you two may as well get in. We are going that way.'

On the way the gentleman asked Liam and Connor about what they expected from their new work. They explained that they were stone masons and quite used to hard work and were looking forward to work in the countryside. Sarah said that she was a cook and looking for work. 'Ah,' he said. 'There is always work for cooks on the site.'

The carriage travelled uphill onto Babylon Lane, then New Road before turning onto Horrobin Lane a narrow farm track which took them over the beginnings of an embankment and a sight that made the Doyle family gasp. To their left and right as far as they were able to see were what appeared to be hundreds of men working with picks and shovels, digging into the valley ground and others with mules and carts carrying away the debris and hard-core to shore up the sides and embankments all around.

The gentleman asked the driver to stop briefly and spoke, 'Look to you right and you see the beginnings of the Lower Rivington reservoir. At the far end is the cart track linking the towns of Bolton and Chorley. To your left is the new Upper Rivington reservoir, beyond that will be the new Anglezarcke reservoir. All this to bring fresh water to the good people of Liverpool and you will be an important part of that.'

Liam said, 'I expected to see new-fangled steam shovels in action.'

'We don't need them. You see those navvies down there. Each one of them can shift at lease thirty tons a day, they are absolutely incredible.'

At the far end of the lane, he dropped them off near the village green saying, 'Sheephouse Lane is in front of you. Go along the lane past the Chapel and you will find your accommodation. Best of luck to you all.'

As they alighted from the carriage and began to walk past the chapel, a young man approached and asked in an Irish accent and a little shyly, 'Are you the Doyle family?'

Liam replied, 'Indeed we are.'

'I am Paddy Murphy and I've been asked to take you to your cabin and to look after you. You must be very important.'

'Why do you say that?'

'You have been brought here by Thomas Hawksley the architect and the top boss who runs this whole site.'

Sarah replied, 'We didn't know who he was, but he was rather kind.'

They entered the family quarters off to the right, behind the chapel. It consisted of two lines of wooden cabins, twenty in all and they had been allocated number five.

Inside the cabin, they saw that it was reasonably comfortable with a wardrobe and cupboards, some cooking facilities, a coal stove, the usual tin bath hanging from the wall and two beds one double and one single.

'We need another single bed,' said Sarah.

'No problem, I'll go and fetch one,' replied Paddy.

While he was away, they began to unpack and settle in. He returned a short time later with a single bed, mattress pillow and blankets.

'What's your job here Paddy?' asked Liam.

'I'm an apprentice stone mason Mister Doyle. I have been asked to look after you and your family and Mister Tetley. Help you to settle in and from tomorrow morning you and Mister Tetley will be my instructors. We are very short of skilled stone masons, and I've been told to show you around the site tomorrow morning, and we start work properly on Wednesday. Where is Mister Tetley by the way?'

'He will be here later. We are getting a little hungry now, is there food to be had?'

'The canteen for families is just across the meadow, you can actually sit down and eat there, but family members who are not employees do not get meal tickets and have to pay for their meals. Another larger canteen is sited down by reservoir workings. That is for the navvies and workforce. They both open at seven in the morning, one in the afternoon and seven in the evening. You take your own plates, knives and forks for the larger one and if you're not there on time it becomes a massive queue.'

Rufus left the train with the Gill family and headed in the opposite direction for a short way, then turned south along a wide cart track into the countryside. When they reached one of the local Blackrod collieries, they went off to the right along a narrow track the locals called Dark Lane. At the top of the hill, they forked left where they found the farm overlooking the Douglas valley.

In the farmyard, Rufus said to the Gills, 'Give me a moment to talk to my sister.'

He went into the farmhouse kitchen where he saw his sister Nora at the table with her head down preparing a meal for her family and the farmhands. She looked up and shrieked when she saw him. 'Rufus, where have you been forever?'

They hugged. 'I'm back in the area now for at least a couple of years. How are you, Bill and the kids?'

'We're all fine.'

'How's mother, that's why I've come back?'

'Not good, she's here with us now.'

Nora took Rufus upstairs where they saw that mother was fast asleep in her bed. They did not disturb her. Back downstairs, Rufus broached the subject of the Gill family who were still waiting outside and explained their needs.

'It sounds Ok,' said Nora. 'We are always on the lookout for good hands, but we will have to put it to Bill. The cottage is vacant. It needs a bit of work but it's liveable. Bill is down at the cowshed now one of our cows is having a difficult birth. Bring Mrs Gill and the girls in and take Mister Gill down there for a chat.'

At the cowshed they found Bill Price, but he was in no mood for chatting. One of his prize cattle, a Hereford was lying on a straw bed obviously heavily in calf and in pain. 'Hi Rufus, nice to see you, talk to you later. This one's been in labour for five hours now and we're getting nowhere fast.'

Bill, who was a small man, lay behind the cow and reached inside. 'I can just about feel the tips of the calf's hoofs, but I can't get far enough in to pull.'

'May I help?' said John. 'I have very long arms, my mother used to say that I should have been an ape, and I have done this before.'

'Who are you?'

'He's a farmer like you,' answered Rufus.

'Ok. Please do.'

John stripped to the waist and lowered himself behind the cow. He felt that the passage was dilated, and he reached inside the uterus. He could easily feel the rear legs of the calf and spoke, 'Yes. It's a breach birth.' He pulled his arm free and asked Bill for a length of rope. Bill knew exactly what he needed and found an appropriate piece.

John made a slip knot and again reached inside, this time holding the rope. He pushed the knot around the hind legs, tightened it and said to Bill and Rufus, 'Pull steadily.' Which they did. 'A little harder now.' And as they did so, he began to feel the calf slide gently towards birth canal. He withdrew and the two men pulled, seconds later a soaking wet female calf slide from the cow. She was rubbed heartily with straw by John who announced, 'Ah she's alive and a lovely one at that.'

Later that day, in the kitchen over a fine lunch, Bill and Nora announced that they would be delighted to employ the whole family. John as a farm hand and Emily and the girls as milkmaids. Bill had a caveat. 'From what you have told me John, and from what I have seen, I am sure that you and your family are looking for your own place eventually and I will do what I can to help you with that.'

At one o'clock that same afternoon, the Doyle's went for lunch at the family canteen. Paddy produced tickets for Liam and Connor, but Sarah and Hannah had to pay. They found the food to be substantial and filled a gap but was not particularly good nor well cooked.

There were only two ladies working there, a middle-aged lady cooking and a young girl serving. There appeared to be no one clearing tables or washing up and the two women appeared to be sweating and harassed. Sarah waited for a quiet period and approached the older lady.

'We are just moving in today and my daughter and I are looking for work. Have you any vacancies?'

'Have you any experience, love?'

'I am a cook, and my daughter is a quick learner.'

'Can you start at five this afternoon to get ready for the seven o'clock tea?'

'You mean dinner?'

'We call it tea, love.'

'What are the wages?'

'Well, you'll be on trial today. If you pass, you'll be on thirty shillings a week and your daughter fifteen. That's six days a week, we get a different staff in on Sundays.'

'See you at five.'

'I'm Molly by the way and that's my daughter Tricia.'

At six the next morning having passed Molly's trial, Sarah and Hannah set off the few yards to work.

At seven, Liam Connor and Rufus were met by Paddy who had arranged to show them around the site and explain things as he knew them.

They set off east along the narrow Rivington and Dryfield Lane cart tracks then turned north to where the long embankment was being constructed along the wider and busier Bolton to Chorley trade route. Even at that time in the morning, there were traders travelling between the towns carrying goods by horse and cart, farm hands and miners, some of them young children walking to their work, and wealthier people going about their business on horseback.

'This is the site of the water treatment works. The purified water will leave here and travel along a thirty-two-mile pipeline which is now under construction between here the town of Prescott near Liverpool. The water will travel by gravity alone and from Prescott will be diverted to various parts of Liverpool. It is intended to correct the spread of diseases such as Cholera Dysentery and other filthy water bourn ailments which are currently rife in the city.'

Rufus spoke. 'You have obviously been doing your homework young Paddy, I'm very impressed. You can be my apprentice Liam already has his.'

They walked on a little further. 'There will be three reservoirs built in three shallow valleys. This will be called the Lower Rivington. Here we are building a long embankment to support this southern side.' They looked and could see navvies deepening the valley and moving the debris to shore up the embankment.

'This reservoir will be fed by the Douglas Springs which are sourced on Winter Hill which you can see in the distance.'

'What is that tower by the hill?'

'Oh, that's Rivington pike tower, it was I am told build about seven hundred years ago when people from the north used to invade this area. It was used as a watchtower and a beacon.'

'As a matter of interest how many of the navvies are Irish?' said Liam.

'About one third of the workforce around one hundred men are Irish.'

They passed the Millstone coaching house and the ancient Headless Cross sign post and turned into Roscoe Low Brow, then Horrobin Lane across which the Doyle's had travelled the day before, and where a high embankment was under construction. They passed a quarry and turned into a lane being newly built on the south side of the Upper Rivington reservoir.

'Local people are beginning to call this the Street Lane. I am told that the name originates from a family called Strete who lived in a manor house along here many years ago. The manor has been pulled down, but it is Liverpool Corporations intention to rebuild it next year. Here is where a pipeline is being laid to feed the local farmers with compensation water as the construction of the reservoir is taking away their natural spring water. It will be fed by gravity like the three reservoirs.'

They picked their way to the end of the lane where the Knowlsley Lane embankment was under construction and Paddy pointed to the final reservoir being built on the other side which was by far the largest of the three this was named the Anglezarke, a name taken from the hill range under which it was located.

'This reservoir will be fed by the river Yarrow. There will be two Watermen's cottages built at either end, one here or the other at the far end on Moor Road. In the hillside high above this reservoir is a small reservoir built about twenty years ago for the people of Chorley, which I believe is called the Bullough. In time to come, I understand that a fourth reservoir will be built also above the Anglezake. Now that's the full extent of my local knowledge. I believe that it is time to attend to our needs at the Moors End public house.'

There was a general nodding of agreement at this last remark.

The next morning onwards they started to earn their pay. Sometimes in the masons' yards, working to plans from the Architect's office. They began the normal twelve-hour shifts cutting stone to accurate measurements for the construction of houses, bridges, waterfalls, and embankments, and sometimes working in the local quarries, extracting and cutting the stone to size before transportation to the site.

Liam and Connor, at Sarah's insistence, whilst working always wore the linen face masks that she made to protect their lungs from the stone dust. Liam noticed with some dismay that most masons did not, including his friend Rufus. Liam challenged Rufus on that issue and pointed out that some of the older masons who were constantly breathing in the stone dust had hacking coughs. One man whom the others called old Joe, had regular coughing spasms even when not working and he looked old even though he was only in his late forties. He clearly had a major problem.

'Sarah feels that you should wear a mask. Will you wear it if Sarah makes one for you?'

'If your lovely wife is so concerned about my welfare then I will wear her mask and I will insist that my apprentice Paddy also wears one if Sarah will so oblige.'

Sarah was happy to oblige and the friendship between the two stone masons and their apprentices flourished.

Other friendships were also being forged. Molly and Tricia Parkinson had become far less harassed since being joined in the canteen by Sarah and Hannah, and the four ladies were swiftly becoming firm friends. They sat drinking tea one afternoon after the lunch time shift and Sarah told the heart-breaking story of the tragedy aboard the SS Londonderry.

Molly Jackson and Tricia were similar in age to Sarah and Hannah and had borne their own tragic moments. Molly told the story of having been brought up in the Blackrod area of Bolton where she received very little in the way of education and from the age of ten years until her marriage to Thomas at the age of eighteen she had worked in the local coal mines first of all as a trapper, opening and closing the wooden trap doors to allow coal tubs to enter and leave the pit, or to allow essential fresh air to enter and circulate. Later as she grew older, she worked as a hurrier pulling and pushing heavy coal-filled tubs along rail lines to be taken to the surface and returning them to the pit face for re-filling.

'Yed daan and keep guin,' she said was the common miners phrase used at the time.

'What does that mean?' said Hannah.

'Put your head down push or pull hard and keep the coal tub moving.'

'That's a terrible abuse of children,' said Sarah.

To which Molly replied, 'I considered myself to be lucky in some ways, before I went down the mine in eighteen thirty, children of eight years were sent to work in the pits. While I was working one day, there was a massive explosion in one of the pits nearby and twelve people were killed. Five of them were girls, one aged just ten years. I know people who are still mourning for their friends and relatives. When Tricia was born, I swore that I would never allow her anywhere near a coal pit.'

'How did you come to be working here?' said Hannah.

Tears welled in Molly's eyes and she spoke, 'Ah. That's another story. My husband Thomas was a coal face worker and just over three years ago he was working at the face when the badly shored roof collapsed on him and he was killed instantly.'

Tricia began to sob, and Hannah went to her and embraced her.

'We then lived in a house owned by the pit owners and rented to us. It took half of Thomas's wages to pay the rent. After the funeral, they told us that we were being evicted as the houses were for pitmen and their families only. I've realised since that is how they got people to work for half pay. We had to leave. We stayed with relatives for a short time until the jobs of cooks came up here and we got living accommodation, and a cabin, like yours with the position.'

Chapter Twelve

Sir Jeffery Fulton was visiting his tenant farmer Bill Price and his wife Nora, they had been working together for many years and were more like good friends rather than employer and employees. Sir Jeffrey was the owner of many acres of land in the area which had included the land he had sold to Liverpool Corporation for the construction of the reservoirs. Following a tour of the farm and over a pot of tea in the farmhouse kitchen he said, 'Everything appears to be going very well Bill, the farms in good shape and the profits are good. Anything to report?'

'Well yes, I have something in mind. Higher Singletons farm on the hillside above the reservoir workings. It's been derelict for about five years now. The old buildings are falling into disrepair and the stone walls are no better. I've been up there cutting hay for the last few years. Hay, I don't really need, and work and I could do without. There's twenty acres of land going to waste.'

'Yes, I am aware of it. I have thought about it quite a bit, but I have not been able to find anyone with the skills and farmer's nous to take it on since old Mister Singleton died.'

'I think that I have found the family that you need. About a month ago, John and Emily Gill came working for me with their three daughters. They are an Irish family over from the problems there. John has become a friend and he is at least as good a farmer as I am, and his ladies are brilliant with animals. I think that they could turn that place around for you.'

'Can I meet John Gill and his family?'

'Yes, I've asked them to stay in their cottage this morning knowing that I was going to make this suggestion. They don't know why, and I think that they are a little concerned.'

Nora made cups of tea for eight and they all sat around the table. The Gill family were relieved when they were told why they were invited into the kitchen and Sir Jeffery was impressed by the Gill family's history and experience and he made the offer. 'But before you make you mind up, I suggest that we travel as a group to the land and buildings and have a look around.'

It was a lovely mid-July day and the eight set of Sir Jeffery with Nora and Emily in his carriage and the rest on a horse drawn cart.

The farmhouse, cow shed, and hayloft were in poor condition with some of the stonework needing repair and some of the stone walls were in a similar state of disrepair. The fields however looked quite good, Bill Price having spent some considerable energy upon them.

John Gill consulted his wife and daughters before saying, 'Sir Jeffery, we will happily take it on and get it back to a full working dairy farm. But I should tell you that it will only be for about two years as it is our intention to travel to the Americas.'

A deal was struck Sir Jeffery realising that he would have to find someone else eventually but hopefully at that stage, it would be as John Gill had described it.

The agreement was that as soon as the place was in a reasonable condition, Sir Jeffery would provide all the farm tools and animals needed.

Even though the house required considerable renovation, the family decided to move in the next day Wednesday where they would have to live rough and ready for a while, and they were able to start work immediately.

Emelia was delighted, the move brought her within half a mile to the cabins where Connor lived.

That same evening at seven o'clock, she was waiting as Connor finished his shift and he invited her to have a meal with him in the canteen. She sat with Liam, Rufus and Connor and related the story of the move to them and how much work they had happily taken on. After the meal, Connor walked back to the farm with her and John took him on a tour of the property. 'It will take us most of the rest of summer to get the place up and running. But I can't tell you how happy we are to have our own place again.'

Connor was of course also very happy to have Emelia close, where he could visit her regularly during the long summer evenings at that time of year. He clearly saw how much work the family had taken on with this project. Slates had fallen from the roofs, doors and gates hanging off their hinges, walls of the buildings and field surrounds were in poor repair falling in places, tracks and paths to and away from the farm were overgrown and neglected. Work, Connor thought that would take the Gill family all the remainder of the summer and some autumn months to complete. He made his way home to his family in a thoughtful mood.

On the following Sunday morning, the Gill family were up early as usual. They had slept well on their straw mattresses, the night had been warm and the morning sunny. John Gills concern was how the family would fare later in the year when the days and nights were cold, and they were unable to retain the heat in this tumbledown farmhouse.

He was repairing the front door to the house when he looked up and saw in the distance two men walking towards him. As they got near, he recognised Liam and Connor. He walked towards the broken farmyard gate to greet them. 'Lovely to see you both, come in and I will make a pot of tea.'

'We haven't come for tea John; we have come to help.'

'You're most welcome there is plenty for you to do.'

As they spoke, three more men who John did not know walked into the yard. 'They are our Irish friends,' said Liam and made the introductions. Before he could finish fifteen of their Irish colleagues rolled in chatting and laughing with each other.

There were now twenty men standing and chatting to each other.

'My God. I don't know what to say,' said John.

As he said it Rufus Tetley walked in with another twelve men. He strode up to John and spoke, 'We are the English squad, awaiting your orders sir.' As he saluted.

'We are all with you for the day,' said Liam. 'Connor has given us a fair idea of what needs to be done. These men are masons, wall builders and joiners at your command.'

'Gentlemen I am at a loss for words. I have no means of feeding so many of you and…' He stopped, embarrassed with a tear in his eye.

Rufus said, 'John, we are all volunteers; we have brought our own food and drinks, we can clearly see without any explanation what needs to be done. You and the girls go about your own work and leave us to it.'

The thirty-three men split into three groups, one to the farmhouse, another group to the other farm buildings and the third to the surrounding walls. Emily, Emelia, May, and Eileen did their best to bring water and friendship to the working men, who were grateful for the drinks and the cheerful female company.

The work carried on all day long until six in the afternoon when without any words of command, work stopped, and the men all assembled in the now neat and tidy farmhouse courtyard.

John and family could not believe the difference. The work they had planned for the next few months of their lives was now complete and they could now open as a working dairy farm.

John spoke to Liam and Rufus, 'They are obviously waiting for something, and I have nothing to give them except my sincere thanks.'

'Please do that they with be very pleased.'

John spoke and his gratitude was plain to see. He said that he and his family would remember this day for the rest of their lives and that each one of them were welcome at the farm at any time and if he could ever repay them for their kindness he would happily do so.

As he finished speaking, more people began to arrive. They were Sarah, Hannah, Molly and Tricia together with the wives and families of many of the men present and they were carrying pots, pans, plates and glasses and a huge amount of food for the assembled, very hungry company.

Two of the men took the fiddles which had been brought to them and began to play Irish country music. Young men placed on the walls large bottles containing clear liquid. 'Is that poteen?' said John to one of the men.

'Ah, it's the good stuff.'

'I'd better warn the English lads they're not used to that powerful drink.'

'Don't worry John. We've watered it down especially for the English.'

'Ok lads. Let's get on and enjoy the Ceilidh.'

Thus the day ended properly with good food and drink, music, singing and dancing. Liam and Sarah noticed that Rufus and Molly seemed to be very taken with each other. The huge six foot plus man and the diminutive woman were together all evening and danced almost every dance. The fun lasted until midnight. Because tomorrow was a working day, the festivities had to end.

As Liam and Sarah walked back to their cabins, they were behind Rufus and Molly. They nudged each other and smiled as they saw the couple were holding hands as they walked together.

John sent a message to his farmer friend Bill Price to the effect that he was ready to open as a functioning dairy farm. One morning later that week, Bill, together with his son Phillip with horse and cart, drove up to the farm and announced that they were awaiting the arrival of Ṣir Jeffery. They were astonished to see how much work had been done in such a short time. John was tempted to tell them that it had been accomplished by great effort by him and his family, but instead said, 'We have some very good friends working on the reservoirs who have helped a little.'

Sir Jeffery arrived midmorning and was equally amazed at the achievement. 'I was clearly right to have great faith in you John, you and your family have done me proud. What we need from you now is a list of the animals and equipment you need to get this place up and running.'

Over convivial cups of tea in the family's makeshift kitchen John said, 'I anticipated your request for a list and here it is.'

'Thank you, John. You keep the list. Here is a promissory note to pay for whatever you need. Phillip is here to assist you with directions and markets. He will then work with you and learn from you. I know that you intend to leave us at some point when I want Phillip to take over. You are the boss until then.'

'Thank you,' said John. 'I now think that while we are all together that we now need to refine our arrangements.' He indicated to Emily to join the group.

Sir Jeffery said, 'Ok I will start. Until you are in production, I will pay the wages of yourself and your family to make this a prosperous enterprise. Once you begin to sell your produce, I will expect a tithe from you.'

'Sorry. What is a tithe?'

'It is ten percent of your profits. That is what all of my tenant farmers including Bill here pay me.'

Bill then chipped in, 'On the understanding that this farm will one day be in the hands of my family and being run by Phillip after you leave, I will provide you with twenty Hereford cows, ten will be already producing milk and the other ten will be youngsters at various stages of pregnancy. The horse and cart we arrived here in is now yours for the duration. Using Sir Jeffery's promissory note Phillip will be working for you and will guide you to the local market to buy all the stools, buckets, churns, tubs, and other equipment you need. I will provide your winter fodder for this season, next season you will provide your own. When you are in production, he will then work for you and be the vender of your goods, he knows the market well. He is being paid by Sir Jeffery now but will then also expect a ten percent cut from your profits. The cows will of course remain my property after you leave.'

John and Emily looked at each other and Emily nodded. They were aware that they were being used by Sir Jeffery and Bill Price. They were also aware of the strength of their position.

'Ok. So we keep eighty percent of our profits from the milk, cheese, and butter we produce. We will of course also be producing calves some of which will later be milking cows and others beef bullocks, if those remain ours at the end of our partnership for us to sell on, we have a deal.'

Sir Jeffery looked at Bill who nodded. 'We have a deal from which we will all profit.'

John and Emily stood and spit on their hands holding them out. Bill and Phillip did the same. Sir Jeffery who was a little more refine, smiled, shrugged his shoulders, and did the same.

There were handshakes all round and that was all that was needed to seal a contract among honest folk.

Chapter Thirteen

On the next Sunday morning, Connor walked out of the cabin early. He knew that Emelia was free that morning and they had planned to go for a walk around the moors of this lovely area. As he did so, he saw Rufus knocking on the door of Molly Jackson. 'Good morning, Rufus.'

'Ah, morning Connor, where are you off to this lovely day?'

'I'm going up to the farm for Emilia and we are going walking trying to learn this part of the world.'

Molly came to the door and heard what he said.

'Why don't you walk with us, we know the area well.'

They set off up Sheephouse Lane to collect Emilia then up the hill and over the footpaths to Rivington Pike, a stone-built tower around one thousand feet up the hillside built on a mound with a wide view of the surrounding countryside on a clear day. It has a view of the Welsh hills and far out to the Irish Sea thirty miles away.

Rufus explained, 'This was built about seven hundred years ago and is one of the beacons to warn local people of raiders from the north hunting in the area. It's quite traditional for local people to walk up to the pike on Good Friday of each year.'

They walked further along towards Winter Hill where they saw several people on the cart track. Molly said, 'This track connects the Bolton and Chorley area with Blackburn to the north, then these West Pennine moors go for many miles north out towards Rossendale and Burnley, pretty barren in parts, mainly for sheep farming really.'

They came to a small tree. 'About ten years ago,' said Molly. 'On this spot, a Scottish man called George Henderson who was a tradesman for a Drapers in Blackburn was walking along this track when he was shot dead and murdered. He was probably carrying money which was not found. A local man James Whittle, who I know, was arrested for the murder but he was acquitted later by the courts, the murder was never solved.'

They started to walk back by a different route which took them downhill through woods and fields until they came to a stone barn.

This time it was Rufus. 'The upper Rivington Barn. This of one of two ancient storage barns which used to be called tithe barns. The other one is just along the lane. Tithe means that the local farmers had to store ten percent of their produce in them for the use of the landowner. They are so well built they will still be around many years from now and believe it or not there was not one nail used in their construction. They are still used as barns, but the tithes have finished. I think that it is easier for the landowners now just to take the money. Well we are almost back home. I hope you found that useful.'

The same Sunday evening, John had invited the Doyle family together with Phillip, Rufus, Molly and Tricia to the farm for an evening meal. He had been with Phillip to the market in Chorley the previous Friday and had purchased all the things he needed, stools, milk tubs, buckets and butter and cheese making churns and other equipment. He was expecting ten milk cows and another ten expectant heifers to arrive from the Price farm the next day and from then onwards his family would be too busy to entertain. He wanted to thank them for all their time and efforts on his family's behalf and was sorry that he could not invite all the people who had assisted.

They had a splendid evening; John had secreted away some of the potent poteen from the previous week. At the conclusion of the meal, Rufus stood and said that he had an announcement to make. The company went quiet. 'Molly and I are getting married a few weeks from now. Tricia has approved and we would like to invite all the present company to our wedding when the arrangements have been made.'

There was a slightly stunned silence for a moment, they had only known each other for a few weeks. This was followed by a rousing cheer and much kissing and back slapping.

'Where will the wedding take place?' said Sarah.

'Well I have spoken this afternoon to the minister at Rivington Church and he says that he can fit us in one Sunday sometime during the next two months and the powers that have said that we can use the site canteen for a wedding breakfast so long as we don't interfere with normal mealtimes.'

'This calls for something special,' said John. He went inside the farmhouse and came back with a bottle of old Irish whiskey. Shouting in a loud voice, 'The water of life, made by Irish monks which I have saved for use and enjoyment on an occasion such as this.'

Molly and Sarah, now the best of friends had tears of pure joy running down their faces.

The next few weeks saw things running smoothly for the two families. Connor and Paddy moved on from simple matters like cutting the rounded copping stones for the wall tops and were now carving the more intricately shaped stones for buildings and bridges to the specifications of the draughtsmen.

Rufus, Connor, Liam, and Paddy all wore masks when they worked and were reminded of the essential need for them when one of the older masons suddenly fell very ill with nonstop coughing. He was forced to cease work and retire to his cabin where a few days later he succumbed and died. He was taken away and a post-mortem examination was carried out which proved that his lungs were totally clogged up and solid with stone dust. This information drifted back to the assembled stone mason group and the requests for masks made by Sarah and Molly became an urgent clamour.

The Gill family were now very busy, milking early morning and evening. The beginnings of cheese and butter making during the day and some nights completely taken up with calving. Before long, all ten pregnant cows had calved and this added to the work with fresh cows to milk and new calves to wean. The family had rarely been busier or happier and Phillip Price was proving a godsend with sales of their produce booming.

Sunday, the 7th of October 1849 was the day of the wedding between Rufus and Molly. At two o'clock in the afternoon of that day, all the assembled guests were in the pews of the beautiful church in Rivington village when the bride entered with her bridesmaids Tricia, Hannah, Emelia,

Mary, and Eileen. The groom and the best man Liam followed shortly afterwards. Rufus had a huge grin all over his face, in fact the grin rarely left his face for the rest of that day.

After the ceremony the guests were headed by Rufus and Molly from the church towards the reception. As they got to the village green they were amazed by the number of various workers, navvies, masons, joiner's canteen staff and others who were waiting to greet them and cheer them on. Rufus until this point had not realised how popular he had become among the various groups of both English and Irish workers, with his cheerful demeanour and sense of humour.

At the wedding feast Sarah brought out a wedding cake she had made secretly, and they were allowed most of the remainder of the afternoon to enjoy the occasion and the meal made especially by the ladies. After the meal the two Irish fiddlers began to play, and Rufus and Molly were clapped and cheered until they were forced to get up and begin the dancing. Sarah was pleased to see that Paddy and Hannah enjoyed every dance and appeared very happy in the company of each other, as did Connor and Emelia. *Hum*, she thought, *do we have other weddings to come soon?*

The celebrations went on until the late afternoon when the Sunday cooks arrived and began to make the evening meal for the workers. The Gill family had to leave quickly. John saying, 'We had better go before the cows burst their udders.'

There was to be no honeymoon. Rufus and Molly were back to work the following morning.

The remainder of that year went without mishap. The two families working hard and saving their money for their eventual journey to the new world.

On Christmas and Boxing Day, the workforce was allowed a rest day to enjoy the season of good will and the two families, including Rufus, Molly Tricia and Paddy met at the farm for a Christmas dinner. It was, they had previously decided time to compare notes and make plans for their eventual departure. After a splendid meal, they sat back and talked. Liam began, 'I have heard from some of my friends at the site that people who have made their way to the Upper Canadian province have done well and have settled in there, perhaps that is the place for us.'

John agreed by saying, 'Yes, and I believe that it is a great place to farm. I think that should be our destination. We will not be ready until the early part of eighteen fifty one that is because the cattle, we own will not be ready for sale until then.'

Liam said, 'There is enough work here for us until then.'

They concluded that the early part of 1851 would be the best time financially for the families to leave and continue with their journey.

That decision having been made they all settled down with a little Christmas cheer, when Conner and Paddy stood up together, they were slightly tipsy and Paddy said, 'Connor you go first.'

Connor said, 'Mr and Mrs Gill. I hope that you don't mind me saying this in company. I would like your permission to become engaged to marry your daughter.'

Emily Gill stood with open arms and embraced Conner saying, 'We have been wondering when you would say that and yes, we are delighted.' John Gill simply had a silly grin on his face.

Paddy chipped in, 'Mr and Mrs Doyle. You may not know it, but Hannah and I have fallen madly in love, and we would also like to become engaged to marry.'

Liam was stunned and had not expected this. Sarah however had seen it coming and she stood as Emily had and embraced Paddy wholeheartedly. Liam however frowned and said, 'Paddy I did not expect this. You must know by now that we will be travelling to Canada soon and we would want Hannah with us.'

Paddy replied, 'Yes sir I know, and I would like to travel with you as Hannah's husband.'

Hannah jumped from her seat and spoke, 'That's what I want too.'

Liam smiled and spoke, 'Then I am delighted for you both!'

Chapter Fourteen

The year 1850 began well and with the prospect of a long journey in the early part of the following year, the two families worked hard, putting as much money aside as was possible. None of the family members ever wanted to travel in a ship by steerage again. It was unlikely that they would ever have enough capital to go first class, so the intention was to travel as second-class passengers when the occasion arose. They were also aware that they would need a good amount of money when they arrived in Canada if they were to prosper there.

The reservoirs were in the final stages of completion that year and many of the navvies who had been on the site for almost three years had moved on to other construction sites, but there was still plenty of work to be done by those left, particularly by the builders, joiners, and stone masons.

Prior to the original reservoir construction beginning a manor house previously owned by the Street or Strete family had been demolished and was to be rebuilt, there were also houses to build for the future water-bailiffs. Liam, Connor, Rufus, and Paddy were kept very busy during this period.

Stone mason's work in the winter months was cold and hard, but much of the stone cutting was done in Lester's and

Horrobin Quarry's near the site which were relatively sheltered from the wind and even though the men were used to the cold, they looked forward to the spring and the warmer weather.

Connor and Paddy were becoming very restless. They had both noticed that some of the site cabins were now empty and would, as far as they were concerned, make excellent honeymoon suites. 'When can we be married?' was the cry.

Liam and John put their heads together. They were basically catholic. They rarely went to mass because of distance and work commitments, but they both agreed that the weddings should ideally take place in a catholic setting.

Phillip Price, the local man had the answer. 'There is a lovely church about five miles away called Euxton Parish Church. It's in the countryside near the manor house itself and a wonderful place for a wedding. I am sure that we can borrow another horse and cart from my dad. We can tidy them up a bit for transport. If you like I will take you both down there on Sunday to make the arrangements. I also know a man who lives at Dill Cottage just round the corner from here is changing it from a shop to a pub-restaurant and intends to call it The Yew Tree Inn. I'm sure he would be pleased to do to wedding feast.'

Liam, Sarah, John and Emily went with Phillip the next Sunday and attended the mass at Euxton Parish Church after which they spoke with the Priest and arrangements were made for the double wedding to take place at two o'clock on Saturday, the 1st of June that year at the Church. It was some months away and the two engaged couples were impatient but delighted by the prospect.

Work carried on as normal with the ten future travellers all saving as best they could for the journey to Canada early the next year.

Time elapsed quickly as time does. The two mothers, Sarah and Emily when they could spare time away from their work duties, competed to make wedding dresses for their daughters, bridesmaids and indeed themselves. The four men in their lives Liam, Connor, John and Paddy took time to find suitable clothing in order not to be too far outshined by the ladies on the special day.

Phillip elected to have the horses and carts spruced up and sparkling for the big day and indeed arrangements were also made for a Ceilidh on the forecourt of the Yew Tree Inn. The landlord saying that he would make sure that good Irish whiskey was available and indeed plentiful on that day.

The big day arrived. It was a beautiful warm sunny day. The Doyle family had been allowed the day off for the wedding and Bill Price had sent men to look after the Gill's farm for the day. The families together with their friends Rufus, Molly and Tricia, and of course the groom Paddy assembled at the farm at lunchtime and awaited their transport to the church. The two brides were hidden away in the farmhouses where their mothers and sisters had dressed them and concealed them from the sight of the men.

Transport arrived and the assembled company were amazed. First to drive into the courtyard was a splendid carriage which John Gill recognised as that belonging to Sir Jeffery Fulton, driven by Phillip Price. Laughing at their bewildered faces, Phillip jumped down from the driver's seat and spoke, 'It's on loan for the day. Sir Jeffery apologises and says that he is too busy to attend personally, and this is his wedding present.'

The two other carts arrived with drivers from the Price farm, Phillip had exceeded himself. The two cart horses were looking at their very best, they had been brushed to a sleek shiny finish and had their manes and tails plaited and hung with flowers. They were wearing their best sparkling brass livery. The carts had cushioned seats fastened to them and were covered with awnings in case of rain. The sides were hung with a silken material and steps were provided in order that the ladies may board and alight with grace.

Phillip said, 'Sir Jeffery thought that the two grooms with the brides' mothers would travel in the carriage to be first at the church to await the brides.'

John Gill took over. 'No, no, no, the carts will go first with the families and guests, Liam and I will then wait fifteen minutes then follow you with the two young ladies in the carriage.'

There was no argument and at twelve thirty the two carts set off for the five-mile journey; several young friends of the two happy couples jumped aboard the carts without invitation and joined the group for the ceremony, happily dangling their legs over the side. Paddy, who had lost his parents to starvation and disease in Ireland and had no one to support him, was probably the happiest man present with friends around him and the prospect of joining a new and loving family.

John and Liam went into the farmhouse where they saw their two beautiful daughters as they had never seen them before in their long flowing white dresses with veils and garlands of flowers. The pair of fathers could barely speak, their throats constricted, and their eyes watered to their respective embarrassment. John had the answer. He produced a bottle. 'The water of life, he managed to mumble, it's my very last one so let us enjoy it.'

Fifteen minutes later, they set off with Phillip driving through the lovely summer countryside to arrive at the church traditionally a few minutes late.

The wedding vows followed by a mass in this beautiful church went without a hitch, the two mothers frequently wiping tears from their eyes. The brides and grooms were sent back on the journey in the carriage with a 'Just Married' sign on the back. The two carts with their joyful load followed waving to all they passed and, in most cases, receiving cheers and smiles back.

At the Yew Tree Inn the Ceilidh began; food and drinks were plentiful, and the two fiddlers were on hand to enhance the celebrations which went on throughout the long sunny evening. For some reason, best known to themselves the two newly-weds disappeared part way through the evening.

Chapter Fifteen

One Sunday the 1st of December that year, the two families had a conference. The building work was winding down and would only last a few more months and John Gill stated that he would be ready to sell his cattle stock in the New Year markets. They realised that although the summers in Canada were warm and comfortable the winters were cold, and they would like as early a start as possible in the year to find and purchase farmland to be ready.

Liam and John would take a few days off work to travel to Liverpool and make arrangements for travel.

The following morning, the pair caught a train to Liverpool. They arrived at lunchtime and decided to go straight to the docks and find Charlie Simms the docks foreman who had been helpful to Connor and who may be able to point them in the right direction.

They found him having his lunch, he remembered them well from Connor's return from Ireland with Emelia and he invited them to dine with him. They explained the problem of wanting to arrive in Canada as early as possible in the New Year. He said, 'So far as I know there will be nothing from Liverpool until later in the year. All I can suggest is that you visit the Glen Line offices just outside the dock gates. They may have something travelling from Ireland, but I warn you they are sometimes called coffin ships, taking the poor, unwanted and sometimes diseased people away from these shores often to their deaths.'

The clerk behind the desk at the Glen Lines office was happy to talk to potential paying travellers, especially when he learned that there were to be ten passengers. 'We have one ship, the Glen Lyon leaving Ross Island, Waterford in Ireland to Montreal in Canada on April the 15th. You will have to make your own way to Waterford, I would suggest that you book on the Liverpool to Dublin Steam Packet well in advance. There offices are just around the corner from here and you can travel by train to Waterford.'

'Why are they called coffin ships?' said John.

'Oh, that's just nonsense it's a perfectly safe way to travel.'

'Will we have cabins?'

'Yes, they are small but comfortable, you will have five cabins with bunk beds, a bench seat and room to store your baggage.'

'How much?' said Liam.

'That depends, do you have any people with you who can cook four are normally required?'

'We do yes, there will be least four skilled cooks amongst us, why do you ask?'

'Well if you are willing to take on the cooking of all meals for the passengers and crew throughout the trip, it will save wages and they will travel free, but they will not be paid you must understand.'

'Yes, I think that we can speak for them, so we will be paying for six.'

'Yes, sixty guineas at ten guineas each, twenty guineas now and the remainder before travel. Take most of your own food on board with you.'

They looked at each other, nodded, paid the man, and received travel tickets.

At the Steam Packet office, they booked for travel on the 10th of April to give plenty of time to get to Waterford.

They set off to find their erstwhile landlady Mr Mullins at her home. She was delighted to see them and invited them in for tea and cake. They explained their position and told her that they would be back in Liverpool for two or three days to purchase food and clothing for the trip, before traveling to Ireland and Canada. Could she find accommodation for ten people?

'Yes, I am sure that I can. Two can stay here with me and I will find places among my friends for the others, please don't worry about that.'

The pair travelled back on the late afternoon train to arrive back at Liam's and Sarah's cabin in the early evening where she and Emily were waiting to hear progress or otherwise. They were delighted to hear the news until John told them of saving money with the cooking agreement.

'So,' said Sarah. 'Who are the cooks?'

'Well,' Liam replied. 'We had in mind yourselves and our married daughters.'

Emily chipped in, 'You can add four other names to that list, and they are all male.'

'But we can't cook,' the two men said together.

'Don't worry about that you'll soon learn.' The ladies retorted.

Early in the February of the new-year, John took his animals to market, his bullocks and heifers in calf were in prime condition for sale. He received the price he was hoping for.

The building work was slowing down on the site. The Street manor house was almost completed as were the watermen's houses on either side of the Anglezarke reservoir.

The families sat together at the farm for a conference about their future and the money they would need to secure that. John began the discussion, 'Before we travel, let us be certain what it is we all want. I have talked of this to Emily and the girls, we eventually wish to jointly own a dairy farm in Canada which will bring about the prosperity of the families, both the Doyle's and the Gill's now that we are so closely aligned.'

Sarah said, 'Hannah and I have agreed that we will be very happy working on a farm and keeping the family well fed and healthy.'

'Connor and I would like to carry on being stone masons,' said Liam. 'But we don't know what the prospects for that work will be. It is likely that our building skills will be needed around any land we may be lucky enough to get to start off with. After that we will have to see.'

'Girls, anything to add?' said John.

'The three of us are happy with farm work and want to carry on with that,' said Emelia.

'Paddy anything from you?'

Paddy blushed slightly embarrassed but very happy to be included. 'I'm with Liam and Connor; I want to help with any building work which needs doing.'

'Right, money. Let's see what we have got at this stage. Paddy, Hannah do you want to start?'

'Yes. I haven't had much time, but Hannah has been saving and we have ninety pounds for the pot.'

'Connor, Emelia?'

'One hundred and fifty.'

'Liam?'

'Four hundred.'

'We have six hundred.'

'By my reckoning,' said John. 'We have a pot of twelve hundred and forty pounds. Well done everybody. I think that we are set to go.'

Their good friends Rufus Molly and Tricia arrived a short time later for a meal with them and to their general delight, he announced that he had just been taken on as general manager in charge of the local quarries and their future in the area was secure.

The next day, John informed Bill Price of the date that they would be leaving the farm and handing over to Phillip. Liam and Connor and the ladies gave notice of their departure to the site authority.

Chapter Sixteen

In the early morning of the 7th of April of 1851, the families rose from their beds and were ready to leave. All preparations and packing having been completed during the previous days. Phillip had now taken over the farm and had sent one of his hands to pick the Gill family up with the cart. Bill, Nora, and Phillip were at the farm gate to wish them well.

It was loaded and they set off for the site cabins to collect the Doyle's and Murphy's. Once they and their baggage were all aboard, they were taken to Adlington Railway Station for the first leg of their long journey.

On loading the baggage onto the train, Liam noticed two large and heavy wooden containers being heaved into the carriage by the Gills. 'What on earth is in those?' he asked John Gill.

'Salted and cured beef that I have been preparing for this journey,' was the reply.

At the Liverpool station, they hired a carriage to take their baggage to Mrs Mullins accompanied by Sarah and Emily whist the rest of them walked.

Mrs Mullins had been as good as her word and there were four of her friends present at the house to take in the families for the next three days until they caught the steam packet ship to Dublin.

They had decided to do some food shopping in Liverpool, but not too much, worried about carrying a large load onto the steam packet and hoped that they could make up the remainder of their travel food in Waterford.

On Thursday the 10th of April 1851, they left a slightly tearful Mrs Mullins to catch the early morning ship the Albert. It was a pleasant day and after heaving their goods aboard, they were able to find seating for the journey which took most of that day. In fact it was during the early hours of the following morning when they arrived in Dublin.

The Railway Station was close to the docks, so they were able to find shelter for the rest of the night on benches inside the station where they managed a little sleep and were able to catch the early train later that morning to their destination of Waterford.

At eight that morning they caught the slow-and-easy, as the newly established train line was dubbed, to Wexford along the east coast, all of them enjoying what may be their last look at their beloved country. At Wexford, they caught the branch line to Waterford Harbour. Arriving in the mid-afternoon the town was quiet, and they were able to find boarding house facilities at a nominal cost for the four days before sailing.

The families were surprised at how easy it was to buy food provisions, even potatoes for the expected six-to-eight-week journey. When they expressed their surprise to one of the market stall holders, he replied, 'It's easy if you have the money if you have not you get nothing.'

On the second day, John and Liam strolled around to the Harbour at the mouth of the Three Sisters River where they found the Brig Glen Lyon already at the quayside. An attempt to board was blocked by a sailor standing by the ramp. 'We are booked to sail with you and were just checking that our booking is in order.'

'Check at the Glen Line office across the way there,' replied the sailor in a not unfriendly manner.

'No problem,' said the clerk. 'You are booked in for ten people in five cabins. Please be ready to board at seven in the morning on the fifteenth with your baggage and food.'

'Who will be our travelling companions?'

'You will be the only paying travellers. There will be one hundred and twenty people in the lower decks. They will be travelling on assisted emigration under the Poor Laws paid for by their landlords.'

Liam replied, 'I've never heard of that, tell me about it.'

'I'm just a clerk here. I value my job so I can't give you my opinion on that, you will have to ask someone else.'

At the appointed time and date, the families were in position at the quayside by the ship to continue with their epic journey towards their goal. They were approached by the sailor John and Liam had previously spoken with and he asked them to remain where they were briefly, and he stood alongside them.

As they waited, a long line of people shuffled towards them. They were obviously very poor people, women, and men of differing ages, some couples with children. Most were thin and hungry looking, some were very poorly dressed almost in rags, others looking a little better dressed and healthy, a few of the younger men and women were even smiling and seemed to be happy to be boarding the ship and leaving the misery they had experienced behind.

Liam spoke to the sailor, 'Are these people the Poor Law emigrants we have heard of?'

'Yea, poor beggars.'

'Why do you say that?'

'Because their landlords are paying their fares and telling them that they are off to the promised-land full of milk and honey, it's cheaper to get rid of them in the short term than keep them here for life. Look how unfit they are, some won't even survive the voyage. Some of those that do have no warm clothing or money. The weather will be fine and warm when we get there but you must experience it to know how cold it gets in the winter. I would predict that by this time next summer half of those boarding will be gone. Our trip in forty-seven was the worst. We boarded a hundred and fifty then and lost a quarter of them of them on the way.'

'Why do you take them?'

'We're a logging ship, the company wants a paying load on the way to pick up our cargo.'

They watched the other passenger's board and when it was completed the sailor told them to board themselves and take their personal baggage. 'We will load your food into the store. I will show you the ropes later.'

On board, they found their five cabins no better or worse than they had expected, just small boarded areas with bunk beds, shelves for their boxes and wall hooks for their clothing and little else.

The sailor they had become familiar with named himself to them as Jed Franks the First Mate. He asked them to accompany him into the galley.

'You will be our cooks for the voyage.' He pointed to four large cast steel stoves. 'Under those are two feet of sand and a row of stones protecting the woodwork below, fire is the greatest danger to us all on a wooden ship. So you must be always careful, whenever the fire it lit someone must be there to supervise.'

'Here is the key to the food and water store. Breakfast should be ready and served at seven in the morning, or six bells, lunch at twelve-thirty or one bell and the evening meal at seven in the evening or again six bells. You'll get used to the naval bell system. I'll have someone prompt you for the first couple of days. Don't forget that you are feeding one hundred and twenty in the hold, twenty crew and yourselves. The crew are hard working men and need much more food than those below decks. We are expecting our first meal from you at six bells today.' Don't worry I will send one of our experienced men to help you today, after that you're on your own.'

'Right,' said Sarah. 'You men oversee flames and stoves; we ladies will do the cooking.' That became to arrangement for the whole trip.

Mid-afternoon, a sailor introduced himself to them as Thomas Crow. He was the ships cook when only the crew and maybe a couple of passengers were aboard on this trip; he was a seaman.

'Thomas,' said Sarah. 'I've been meaning to ask. Where are the ships toilets?'

'Ah you mean the heads. They are in the ships bows over the sea where the wash from the ship keeps them clean.' He laughed and spoke, 'But you don't need to use them you have been provided with slop buckets to use and to throw over the side.'

The families knew that they had to learn quickly how to cook in and serve from the massive hanging metal cauldrons, buckets and containers of the ship's galley. 'This will be easy,' said Thomas. 'The ship is not moving, wait until you are cooking at sea.'

Together they made a thick creamy burgoo stew for the crew, which Thomas Crow watered down for the occupants below decks.

Late afternoon, the captain ordered up-anchor which took a little while as they were fouled with weed and with the aid of pilots, they were escorted from the Suir and Barrow rivers into the Waterford Estuary from where the captain set sail north along the east coast of Ireland. As it went dark that first day, the passengers were thrilled to see coastal house lights in the distance. The winds were light, the sea calm and the ship were rocking gently, but even so some of the people new to the sea were violently sick, other felt slightly queasy.

Food was served at six bells. The sailors who were free ate heartily, most of the others ate sparingly because of the motion of the ship.

The Gill's, Doyle's and Murphy's had an early night knowing that they were due to rise at three bells to start preparing breakfast. Liam and John were first up to light the stove fires after which they roused the ladies and went back to bed.

On the first day, there were a few complaints from sailors who were not interested in an oat and saltwater gruel but wanted more of the stew they had enjoyed the day before. The ladies soon got used to what to cook and when and after a few days the family even began to be happy with the routine which gave them things to do other than just watch the coast slip by.

It took just three days to reach the northern part of Ireland and the travellers were delighted to be able to see from port side the norther shores of County Antrim and to the starboard the coastline of Stanraer and the Mull of Kintyre in Scotland before the ship finally entered the Atlantic Ocean.

The light wind became even lighter, and the ship was almost becalmed. The captain ordered that handheld fishing lines with multiple hooks be distributed among some of the passengers to augment the food supply. Paddy and Connor and some of the young men from the hold took up the challenge, none had ever fished before. The captain clearly knew this part of the sea well and the mackerel began to flow aboard in their hundreds, enough to feed the whole ships company for the next two days.

Eventually the winds increased, and the ship was in the full Atlantic Ocean away from the shores and moving westward at a good pace. This, of course, meant that the ship was now swaying and rolling much more violently than previously creating seasickness on a scale not experienced before. The smells emanating from the below decks due to seasickness and diarrhoea were now difficult for the families to bear.

Early one morning in the second week of the voyage, Liam and John were just finishing lighting the stove fires when the captain walked into the galley. They had not spoken to him before, he was a short stocky Scot. He had always appeared to be gruff and dour to the two friends, but this morning he seemed friendly enough. 'Any chance of a pot of tea gents?' he spoke.

'No problem,' replied John.

'You may know by now that we are basically a logging ship on our way to Canada for our main cargo. We are forced by the company to take the poor people in the hold to offset the cost of the outward journey. Please don't think for a moment that the crew and I have no care for these people, we have no choice but to take them.'

For a moment, John was reminded of his days farming in Ireland when he had seen his produce, with the instructions of the landlord exported or sold to merchants in the cities rather than go to feed the impoverished. Whenever that thought came into his head, he felt a similar shame to that obviously experienced at this moment by the captain.

'I have just heard that one of the older men has become very ill. I am hoping that it is not typhus or something nasty. Have any of your people any medical or nursing experience?'

They then knew that the captain was not visiting them just by chance, he clearly had a mission.

Liam said, 'We have been forced in the past to nurse our own parents and family through serious illness and death, but we are by no means medics of any kind.'

'Would you do me great favour, will you go into the hold and look at this man and let me know what you think.'

Liam picked up one of the galley lanterns and spoke, 'Finish your tea. I will go now and report back in a few minutes.'

Before ascending to the hold, he went to him cabin and placed one of his stonemason's masks on his face. 'What are you doing?' came the voice of Sarah, as she rose from her bed to prepare herself for cooking duties.

'I'll tell you later,' replied Liam.

As he approached the steps to the hold, he could smell the dreadful aroma of human waste and hear the deep moans of someone in great pain.

He entered the hold and made his way past hammocks and bunks of sleeping humanity towards a corner from which the sound emanated. There he saw a family. The older man was lying on a blanket, moaning, and gasping for air, he clearly has great difficulty breathing. Liam held the lantern towards him, and he saw that the man's face was red, swollen and covered in hives. He was scratching away at his face and hands and upon realising that there was someone around, he pleaded for water.

The two younger people, a man and woman, near to him awoke to the light and to his cries and Liam heard a child begin to cry.

Someone from across the way shouted, 'Can you please shut up we're trying to sleep here.'

The young woman said, 'He's my dad. He started to feel ill a few days ago, not long after we boarded. We are trying to look after him but now we don't feel that well ourselves.'

Making his way back to the galley, Liam was feeling great guilt in that he had not been able to make any attempt to help the family.

In the galley, Sarah and Emily had started the preparation for the ships breakfast. The captain was still there chatting with John and the ladies.

As he entered, they all looked at Liam expectantly. 'Well captain, you know that I am not qualified to tell you this, but I believe that the man you sent me to see has typhoid fever I have seen it in the past. I also believe that he may have passed it on to his daughter and her husband. There is also a young child who may also have it. It is my opinion that they should be isolated away from the others in the hold before its spreads.'

The captain's head dropped, and he looked totally crestfallen as he walked from the galley, he said, 'I will ponder upon it with the first mate, and we will see what can be done.'

Later that same day, the captain again came to the galley where he found Liam and Paddy lighting the stoves for evening meal. 'Thanks for what you did earlier we have found an isolation space in a small holding area just below decks that we don't use much. They are as comfortable as we can make them, one of the ladies in the hold Mrs Sheehan, who was a nurse and knew the family before they came aboard has undertaken the job of keeping them fed, watered and as clean as she can. She is also isolated in a small room next to them.'

'But there's a "but" coming, isn't there? You're a busy man and you haven't come down here just to tell us that, have you?'

'You're a mind reader, Liam Doyle. Yes, they have a young boy, almost a baby and he does not appear to have the disease. He is with Mrs Sheehan now, but she is too busy to look after him. I wondered…'

Liam was about to reject the idea when Paddy stepped in, remembering his own past, losing his parents at an early age and being brought up reluctantly by other family members.

'Yes. Hannah and I will take him. I hope that his parents recover, and we will look after him until they do.'

'You're taking a risk,' said Liam, 'if he has the disease, he might pass it on to you.'

'I'll speak to Hannah now. If she agrees, we're doing it.'

Thus, however temporarily the family gained a new member.

Chapter Seventeen

The ship was now sailing into a brisk headwind and to gain headway, they began the skilful manoeuvre of tacking. This taking up the energies of the sailors completely changing the ship's course every half hour. The ladies decided that they would need feeding well that evening.

The captain's early morning visits ostensibly for pots of tea became a regular occurrence. At first the families wondered why, until he explained that he enjoyed and could relax in their company. At sea he was the only disciplinarian among a crew who without strict authority could take control and may even act as men had in bygone years, taking over the ship and its contents and selling them at a foreign port to the highest bidder.

This was the last voyage of the old brig Glen Lyon, he said. The company was now updating to iron steam ships. He was now in his sixties, and it was his intention, he told them, to retire at the end of this voyage to his cottage just outside Edinburgh and live off his pension. He was very much aware that the ladies were feeding the passengers below far more than they had been allocated by the company and he was happy with that. Far too many had died in previous years due to company penny pinching. He wanted this to be a comfortable journey for as many as possible and to retire a contented man.

'If we have to buy more food for our return journey, the company won't be pleased by the bill, but I will be on my way to Scotland by then.'

Three weeks into the voyage, the hold passengers were better fed and feeling the benefits of regular and substantial feeding. They were also becoming organised and had transformed the hold into a much more agreeable living space, with family units able to live together and toilet buckets regularly emptied, cleaned, and screened off with curtains in accordance with gender.

They had also elected a small committee to see to their welfare; Diarrhoea was still a prevalent problem, creating an all-prevailing stink. Their food was well cooked but the water they were receiving was smelly and scummy. They believed that to be the source of the illness which could, if left uncontrolled, lead to dysentery and death. Two people Sean and Nancy McMahon were asked to approach the captain and ask for a remedy.

The captain had always appeared to be remote dour and unfriendly to the downstairs passengers and neither Sean nor Nancy held out much hope of an interview, let alone a solution. They were surprised when the captain not only agreed to a meeting but invited them into his cabin for a glass of wine.

They explained their problem and the captain nodding his head shouted to a passing sailor, 'Jack, please ask Sarah Doyle to step into my cabin.'

The problem was reiterated to Sarah who immediately said, 'I believe that water from the barrels to be the source of the illness, it was not good to begin with but has increasingly become worse. I pre-boil all our family water the day before. I think that may be our solution. A lot of water will be involved to keep over a hundred people from thirst. It can be done, but we will need people from the hold to help.'

'We want to help,' said Sean. Several of the ladies would love to give hand with the cooking and we also have a few young men who would dearly enjoy working around the ship.

'What about the sailors' water?' said Sarah.

'Ah, we have our own methods,' was the reply.

The captain pontificated. 'Sarah I will leave organising the boiling of water and cooking to you. Sean I will speak with the mate Mr Franks; he will let you know what work is required around the ship. I think that we are done.'

The Monday morning of week four arrived and it was becoming clear that boiled water going to the hold was having a beneficial effect on the digestive systems below decks. The smell emanating was not exactly pleasant, but less awful that before. The new system appeared to be working.

The winds had changed and were now blowing steadily from the east and the ship was making good progress, and all seemed well.

Sarah and Emily having finished cooking breakfast and clearing away decided on such a lovely morning to take stroll around the decks when they met the captain and first mate in the company of Mrs Sheehan walking towards them. The two men doffed their caps and walked on. Mrs Sheehan stopped for a chat.

'How are your patients Mrs Sheehan?'

'Mr Regan died during the night. It was a blessing; he had suffered so much, and his daughter Cathy and son-in-law

Mark are very ill. They are asleep and comfortable now. I don't expect them to last much longer. That's why I am here, we have just had a burial at sea service held by the captain and mate.'

The ladies were shocked. 'We have walked near to the isolation area a few times and heard no cries. We thought they were on the mend,' said Emily.

'The captain has been very good. He brought me a jar of laudanum a few days ago which he had been saving for such an occasion and I have been able to administer it to them and keep them comfortable in their final days.'

As they were talking, Paddy and Hannah walked towards them. Paddy was holding the child in his arms. 'Oh, I'm so glad that Mickey is still well,' said Mrs Sheehan. 'I had so hoped that you would not bring him to me ill, he will be alright now, if he had typhus, it would show itself by now, babies are so resilient.'

'Mickey,' said Hannah, 'we did not know his name. We will keep him well until he can be re-united with his Ma and Pa.'

'I am sorry dear but that won't happen, I don't expect them to last for more that another couple of days.'

'Whatever happens,' said the slightly shocked Paddy. 'This child will have a good home.'

Hannah then said tearfully, 'Please let us know about Cathy and Mark, if they are to be buried at sea, we will bring Mickey along so that we can tell him in the future that he was with them when they left.'

Two days later, the pair were asked to be on the aft-deck at ten in the morning. They arrived with Mickey to find that the two bodies were wrapped together in a canvas sailcloth and had been placed on a temporary structure above the sea.

The only other people present were the captain, the mate, two sailors and Mrs Sheehan. The service was short but respectful Mrs Sheehan led the prayers, pleading for the souls of the two people who had died so young. The captain concluded the service by committing the bodies to the deep and asking for god's mercy on their souls. He nodded to the sailors who cut the rope holding the bodies, which slid down from the structure and entered the sea sinking out of sight immediately.

The captain concluded by saying, 'I sincerely hope that I never have to do that again.'

As they walked away together, Mrs Sheehan told them that she was travelling to live with her son and his family who lived close to Montreal, she was hoping that they would be at the Wharf to meet her on arrival. Joseph was her only son who had travelled alone to Canada five years before and had flourished. He now had a wife and two small children. The captain had been very good to her and had allowed her to remain in the cabin for the remainder of the voyage. Hannah told her that if she wanted company at any time, she was always welcome in the galley.

They had been at sea a month when passengers excitedly saw land to the starboard side. 'We are almost there,' was the general cry only for sailors to dispel that notion by telling them that they could see the coast of Nova Scotia and that the ship was about to sail between there and Newfoundland to enter the Gulf of St Lawrence, they were still at least two weeks from their destination.

It was hard for people who were until then natives of small island countries to imagine the immense size of the land they were about to enter.

Once inside the gulf, the winds became quiet. They were making progress but slowly. The captain decided that it was time for more mackerel fishing. Out came many hooked lines, there were plenty of volunteers. That day Connor alone pulled in eighty fish of stunning quality. The pleasure of the evening meal that day was intense after the daily menu, however well-cooked of oat gruel, burgoo, salted beef stew and ship's biscuits.

The next day held no time for such frivolities, the wind picked up but came from the wrong direction and the sailors became involved again in the backbreaking process of tacking the ship.

They were seeing more and more vessels mainly French fishing boats, but some sailing ships were heading towards the ocean, and they occasionally saw a metal plated steam ship, the captain looked upon these enviously and was heard to say, 'They don't have the problem of tacking with the wind, the crew must have a very comfortable life.'

At one point, they were tacking when they approached a large island. 'Anticosti,' said the captain. 'We need to steer well clear of her, she is surrounded by reefs and rock which will sink us if we get too near.'

Whilst the tacking was hard going for the sailors, the passengers enjoyed it because it gave them the opportunity to see both sides of the now-narrowing gulf before they entered the river itself.

Because of the closeness of the shores, the danger of rocks and the great number of passing ships they were again to the relief of the passengers forced to anchor at night which of course meant that the ship was in calmer waters and sleep came easier.

On the morning of their fifth week at sea, the ship entered the St Lawrence River which was forty miles wide at that point. They had not travelled far when a very smart looking schooner sailed in their direction and hailed them. It was not unexpected, and the St Lawrence River pilot came aboard. He was a genial French Canadian named Alexis Barbet, who could speak good English and he would be with them until they were able to dock at Montreal which was yet some days away. He knew the river well and would steer the ship at times and advise the captain to overcome any dangers they may face.

When he boarded at first, he thought that it was purely a freight carrier, when he realised that it was carrying poor law passengers his face fell, he had often seen and heard of the disease that such ships carried and was obviously concerned for his own safety and that of his family. However following a visit below decks and seeing for himself the relatively good general health of the passengers, there he was a much happier man.

The pilot served papers and a pamphlet upon the captain ordering him to sail to Grosse Island near Quebec where all passengers and crew would be subject to examination by doctors before being allowed onto the mainland of either Canada or America. Anyone found to be sick in any way would be forced into isolation on that island until the doctors deemed them well enough to enter. The captain was in any case familiar with the requirements.

The winds were favourable at first and they sailed on, soon they were close enough to the southern riverbank to see into the distance. Whenever the pilot was free, he was happy to point out names of the many white painted villages on the banks on that side of the river and the variety of contributory streams and rivers entering the St Lawrence. There were many other places of interest to charm and fascinate the passengers. They could see Mont Camille on the southern shore and many tree lined hills and verdant valleys.

The wind again shifted, and they had to re-commence tacking bringing into view the northern shore and its equally beautiful scenery. As they lay at anchor in St Pauls Bay about fifty miles from Quebec on the north side of the river, they were able to see a beautiful island which Alexis called the Isle aux Coudres. He said that the rivers Du Gouffre and Des Marees flowed into St Pauls Bay after meandering through valleys between mountains' way to the north.

The May weather was warm and sunny and passengers, whenever they were allowed, were very happy to sit out and enjoy the views during the days it took to sail from the gulf to Grosse Island. It began to dawn on some the immense size of the land of their future. They had sailed almost the full length of Ireland in less time than it had taken to reach the immigration point from the gulf, let alone travel into the interior.

The ship anchored at Grosse Island on the 30th of May 1851. Then began the long wait for a doctor to board the ship and free them from isolation. Orders were issued for a thorough general cleaning of the whole ship by the crew and passengers alike in preparation for the coming medical inspection. All aboard were expected to wash themselves and wear clean attire.

The captain during this waiting period still visited the galley in the early morning whilst the stove fires were being lit for the day's cooking.

'How long will we be here?' John asked.

'Until one of the doctors decides to visit the ship and give us all clear to leave. I am not flying a blue flag which should tell them that we do not believe we have any contagion aboard. It's the first time I have been able to do that, and I am unaware of how they will perceive that, will it bring them quicker or will is slow them down. I do know that they are dreadfully short of medical staff.'

'What can you tell you about the island?'

'Grosse Island. It simply means "large island" in French. It has been the quarantine station for some years now. The aim is to stop disease from entering Canada or North America. It does not always work. I am aware that Montreal has suffered much from cholera and typhoid brought in by emigrants and has a large Irish graveyard. In the past, particularly in 1847, Grosse Island was completely overwhelmed; there were so many sick that people were left to live or die on the ships that brought them. Others were taken to the island where they were left in tents and sheds with no one to give them even the basics like fresh water.'

'How many Irish people do you think have perished during these awful times?'

'It is estimated that there are three thousand Irish graves on the island and in my opinion at least that number again were buried at sea.'

Sarah and Emily entered the galley. Sarah had a question. 'Is the water here fresh or saline?'

'The water here is not saline, but please don't drink it. Can you see all the ships anchored here awaiting medical inspection? They are all cleaning and throwing out their filth into the water, some of that filth will be diseased and we don't want to bring that aboard our ship.'

It was several days before the doctor boarded the ship. The captain was sure the reason was that they were carrying poor law passengers and, even though he was not flying a blue flag the island doctors probably feared the worst.

On the 5th of June, they saw the doctor's vessel approach and the doctor boarded alone. The doctor insisted upon checking the passenger list when boarding and comparing that with the numbers now to be examined. 'It seems that you have lost only three people during the voyage. Is that true?'

'Yes, and I believe that was three too many,' replied the captain.

He was escorted by the captain to the hold where he expressed surprise at the cleanliness and the not too unpleasant smell.

He examined the passengers one by one. Checking their heart rates, breathing capacity, and looking inside their mouths. He also checked each crew member, including the captain and mate, before issuing a certificate allowing them to progress.

Before leaving the ship, he approached the captain. 'You are to be congratulated on the cleanliness of your ship and the health of your passengers. That is the first time I have made that comment to the captain of a poor law ship.'

Chapter Eighteen

Very early the following morning before daylight and the weighing of the anchor, the captain and Alexis were in the galley for their now regular early morning pot of tea.

'Where to now captain?' enquired Liam.

'Montreal. That is where we will take our leave of you sadly, I have enjoyed your company and your care for others and hard work. We will take on board our logging cargo there and head back to Liverpool. My very last trip on the ocean,' he said with a pensive smile.

'What can you tell us about Montreal Alexis? Will we be able to dairy farm in that area?'

'It is the city of my birth, and I would not recommend it for dairy farming. Montreal is a mountainous island. Mount Royal was how it got its name. It has been occupied for many centuries by the indigenous Iroquoins. One hundred years ago it was just a fortress. Now it is a French speaking city and the centre of the fur trade. I would suggest that you travel further along the river perhaps to Kingston which is English speaking and where dairy farming would be more likely to succeed.'

They up-anchored that same morning to sail the two hundred miles from the east of Grosse Island to Montreal. Once clear of the island, the captain gave permission for fresh water to be taken on board and to the relief of the family, they were able to cease the onerous morning water boil.

They were approached by Alexis during the voyage and asked how long they intended to stay in Montreal. John told him that they were unsure, maybe one or two days, their cash supply was still good but finite and they had a need to move on and find suitable farming land before it began to dwindle.

'Even for a short time, my friend I will be happy to find you good but reasonable priced accommodation and to show you around my beautiful city.'

The weather was good the wind was fair, and the scenery was beautiful. The family were still working hard for the few days it took to complete the last part of the journey on board the Glen Lyon. They were generally content but a little apprehensive about their uncertain future.

On the fifth day as they approached the Montreal wharf, Sarah and Emily were standing alongside Mrs Sheehan and were able to share with her delight when she saw her son standing in the distance waiting to greet her. Most of the passengers were silent and a little glum, sharing the apprehension of the families.

It was late on a Saturday when the ship anchored at the wharf, once it was safe and the ramp had been lowered into position, the passengers were instructed to disembark. Mrs Sheehan was happy to do so and almost ran down the ramp into the waiting arms of her son. Others left the ship reluctantly. They had been well fed and made reasonably comfortable aboard. To their surprise and delight, they were greeted by an Irish group of well-wishers who gave them advice on where to find accommodation or work in this industrial city, or for those who planned to move on elsewhere, advice on travel.

The families who now numbered eleven as no one had come forward to make a claim on Mickey and he was now the unofficial son of Paddy and Hannah, after taking leave of the captain and wishing him well in his retirement, they moved forward to take whatever travel information was available. They were informed that the next steam ship to Kingston would leave at noon on the Monday. They were advised to attend the Royal Mail offices on the Quayside to book passage.

As they left the office having booked tickets at the cost of ten shillings per person, they were greeted by Alexis. 'I thought that I had lost you, how long are you staying in Montreal?'

'Until noon on Monday,' replied Liam.

'I promised that I would look after you and I will. You need two nights' accommodation and food. Do you mind roughing it a bit?'

'We've had plenty of practice,' said John.

'Come with me.'

They walked a short distance until they came upon a smart row of stone-built houses and a large stable block. Alexis, who was part owner of the stables, spoke briefly to Jacques his co-owner, then said, 'Above here is a hay loft. It is warm and clean and comfortable; will you be happy sleeping there for two nights? Before you answer please look.'

It was as he had described, clean and comfortable and the families were very pleased.

'You ladies have fed and looked after me for more than two weeks and I will be delighted to look after you. Please come to my house at the end of this row in one hour and we will dine.'

Thus the families were made to feel well received in this land which felt new and wonderful to them.

The next day, again after being fed and watered, Alexis took the eleven on long and tiring trek to the top of Mount Royal where, from this vantage point they could get a view of the whole city. The day was clear and they could even see the mountains of Vermont across the river in the far distance.

Alexis pointed out the Notre Dame Basilica in the near distance and spoke, 'That's where we are going next.'

Two hours later, they entered the Basilica to find a mass being said in Latin which they all understood and were pleased to attend. After the mass, they were able to walk around and admire the building which had been under various stages of construction since sixteen fifty-two and was still by no means complete. Liam and Connor on seeing this were tempted to stay in Montreal as stone masons and to become a part of this enormous task. When they voiced this, they were reminded by Sarah that doing so would split up the families and that was not the purpose of this huge joint undertaking. In any case, Montreal was French speaking and not one of them understood a word.

That evening they were treated to genuine French hospitality, a meal in Alexis's extensive garden with his family and French speaking neighbours. The wine flowed, and the main entertainment of the evening was people laughing at each other's efforts to understand others by using gestures and pulling grotesque faces to get points across.

Well before noon the next day, they bade farewell to Alexis and boarded the paddle steam ship Magnet to travel the one hundred and eighty miles to Kingston. The ship was a postal service and there were various stopping points on the journey which took five days to complete. They were able to buy the food they needed in the ship's canteen, and they were allocated a sleeping area with hammocks. With no one to describe the areas through which they passed the families simply enjoyed the scenery which was as rich as any they had previously seen on the now narrowing banks of the St Lawrence River.

John encountered on board a local solicitor Michael O'Sullivan traveling back to his hometown of Kingston after a working trip to Montreal. He told John that his parents brought him from Ireland twenty years before and they had settled in Toronto where he had received his education. After chatting for a while, John told him of their plans of building up a dairy farm in the area. He was advised to visit the Town Hall and ask for the Agriculture Department where he may find some assistance. He informed John of the location of his office in case the families should need any further help.

On arrival at Kingston situated just to the northwest of Lake Ontario, they found it to be a quiet and peaceful town. It was early morning and they checked in overnight at two very reasonably priced riverfront boarding houses.

John called the families together in the lounge of one of the houses and spoke, 'Right I believe that we should now check what money we have remaining after out long journey to get to this point.'

A count revealed that they had one thousand pounds sterling left from the original twelve hundred and forty pounds.

On the Monday morning, John and Liam elected to take the remaining money to the local Bank of Kingston, because of the large amount of cash and the fact that they were new customers. The pair were invited into the manager's office.

'Ah,' said the manager. 'One thousand pounds sterling, let me see. We are still operating with Canadian pounds; we are soon to convert to dollars to comply with our American neighbours.'

He made a calculation. 'Your money converts to one thousand one hundred and sixty-five Canadian pounds. It will still have approximately the same purchasing power as a similar amount back home. Do you wish to bank all of that?'

The pair had a quiet discussion. 'No, we will bank one thousand and keep the rest for expenses.'

Outside the bank they were jubilant. 'We have travelled all that way, ten of us, sorry eleven, for thirty-five pounds.' They quipped almost together. It was still early afternoon, so they decided while they were up on their luck to try the Town Hall. The receptionist listened to their wishes and following a call, booked them an appointment for ten the next morning to be interviewed by the head of the Agricultural Department and his staff.

Back at the lodgings, the rest of the families were equally delighted by their financial good fortune and spent a very pleasant first evening – their first in Upper Canada and hoped for good fortune the next day.

Just before the appointed time, all eleven trooped into the Town Hall. The receptionist said, 'Sorry the Department will only interview four of you, you choose which four.'

John, Emily, Liam, and Sarah were chosen and entered the chamber. Samuel Jenkins introduced himself as the head of the department, and after the introductions were competed, he said, 'Are you all farmers?'

'No,' said John, 'Emily, myself and our three daughters are farmers.'

'And you?' said Jenkins looking at Liam and Sarah.

'I and my son and son-in-law are stone masons and builders and Sarah here and our daughter are cooks.'

'Yes. I see the relevance, builders, particularly stone masons are in great demand. John and Emily may I introduce Mr Arnold and Mr Wright. They have great dairy farming knowledge, and they will interview you. Mr and Mrs Doyle would you please step outside for a short while, and would you ask Mr Gill's daughters to step in.'

They did so and joined the rest of their family to wait with bated breath for the next thirty minutes, at which time Mr Jenkins came to them and spoke, 'Will you all come into the chamber now? We have made a decision and would like you all to be present to hear our findings.'

They entered the chamber to find that ten seats had already been arranged in two rows before a desk. Mr Arnold and Mr Wright had departed and a younger man who Mr Jenkins introduced as Wayne Taylor was in their place.

'First of all,' said Mr Jenkins. 'John Gill and family have passed our test with flying colours. In fact their examiners admitted that they know more about dairy farming than they do. We have an offer to make. On the banks of Millhaven Creek, near the town of Odessa about twenty miles east of here, we have a two hundred and fifty acre site which I am told is perfect for dairy farming. Six years ago, we allowed a man called Jake Morris and his family to take the site, without payment on the clear legal understanding that within five years it had to be a dairy farm, much needed in the area to serve the local flourishing population. Otherwise the land would be forfeit. No such farm exists. We have served notices on Mr Morris and his family to quit the land, only to be threatened by him with a firearm.'

'Is Morris a dangerous man?' asked Emily.

'Before being served with papers and asked to leave the land, he had been regarded as a hardworking gentleman.'

Liam interrupted, 'Are you saying that we can take this land without payment in a similar way?'

'No I am afraid that those days are past but under these difficult circumstances, we will sell the land to you at a very nominal price but with a similar caveat, you must have a fully functioning dairy farm serving the area within five years or we will take it from you.'

'What does the word caveat mean?'

'That it will be subject to a legal agreement.'

'What is a nominal price?' said John.

'Five hundred Canadian pounds. Under normal circumstances it would cost you many times that.'

'Can we please discuss this before we commit?'

'Of course we will leave you for a short time.'

The two men left the chamber. The families sat around, and it did not take very long for them to arrive at a unanimous decision that it was too good an opportunity to discard.

Mr Jenkins and Mr Taylor returned, and it was agreed that the deal would go ahead.

'We will need tomorrow to draw up the contract and it will be ready for signature on Thursday morning. Here at ten please with cash or your banker's draught for five hundred pounds.'

Wayne Taylor chipped in, 'The farmland is about twenty miles from here. You will need transport to get you there. I will be accompanying you to start the eviction process of Jake Morris and family. I suggest that we meet up tomorrow morning at ten o'clock at your boarding house and begin to make some arrangements.'

The next morning, Wayne arrived at the lodgings in a very smart buggy pulled by a young and very handsome horse.

'I've been asking around,' he spoke. 'And I understand that a local wheat farmer just outside town has a covered waggon and two mules for sale. The waggon will be well used, and the mules won't be youngsters, but I believe them to be in reasonable condition and at a good price. I think this will be something you will need over the next few weeks as the land is a few miles from the town, and you may need somewhere to sleep for a while. Interested?'

'How much?' said John.

'He is asking one hundred and fifty pounds, but they have been for sale for a few weeks, and I think the price can be negotiated, I will take you to see the owner if you wish.'

'Let's go.'

John and Liam set off with Wayne in the buggy through the town and into the countryside. An hour later, they pulled into the courtyard of the wheat farm. Wayne got out and approached the farmer who having seen them enter his yard was walking back towards them from the fields.

'Mister Mahoney,' said Wayne. 'I understand that you have a pair of mules and a waggon for sale.'

'I do indeed would you be the potential purchaser?'

'No the gents behind me.'

John heard the clear Irish accent and cogitated. 'This might be harder than I thought.'

'Mister Mahoney I am a fellow Irishman. We have just arrived in Kingston and wish to start a dairy farm. So we won't be in competition with you. Your mules and waggon may help us get started, but we have a limited amount of money.'

Craigie Mahoney's also noted the accent, his eyes narrowed he could also see a bartering session coming up. He had a new waggon and two younger mules, the old waggon was obstructing his barn and he was having to find food for the older mules for no reward.

They entered the stable. The mules were together in a loose box. John entered to examine them. They were obviously of middle age but in quite good condition, they probably, he thought had five or even six working years ahead of them.

In the barn he was able to inspect the waggon. It had certainly seen much better days; it was dirty and displayed damage to various parts of the woodwork and the canvas covering was torn in places. He paid particular attention to the wheels and hubs and found them to have been well maintained. 'It would do the job required of it he had no doubt.'

'Ok, what's the verdict?' said Mahoney.

'The mules are getting on a bit and the waggon has seen better days, but I am willing to pay one hundred for the lot.'

Mahoney looked aghast. 'What part of Ireland do you come from?'

'County Mayo.'

'My mother used to say they were all robbing villains from County Mayo, the price is one hundred and fifty.'

'It doesn't look as though we can do business today,' said John. He started to walk away towards the barn door.

'Wait. I'll go along with one twenty-five.'

'One fifteen and that is my final offer and I want harness and reins included, take it or leave it.'

Mahoney smiled and spoke, 'To help fellow Irishmen prosper in this land of their choice I will take one fifteen, even though you are robbing a poor compatriot of his livelihood.'

The two men laughed spat, on their hands and shook them. Both happy with the outcome.

John and Liam sat aboard the waggon with John driving and following an incredulous Wayne back to their lodging all three happy and laughing.

The ladies immediately fell in love with the two mules and made a great fuss of them. They did not however love the dilapidated waggon. When they were told that it may well be their new home for a few days whilst something better was constructed, they set about cleaning it and repairing the torn and damaged canvas covering.

Wayne took the two mules away until they were needed saying that he would groom, feed them and have them in good condition for the journey.

At ten the next day, John and Liam were back at the chambers where Mr Jenkins produced the contract for signing. John however was suspicious, his mind went back to Rivington where he had spent two years developing a flourishing dairy farm, only to lose it. He was determined that he would not spend five years developing another to have it snatched away.

He remembered his brief encounter with Michael O'Sullivan on the steamer and his promise of help in it was needed.

'Would you both please sign the document at the bottom of the last page?' said Jenkins.

'Will you give us a short time to take it away and check it over?' John replied.

Liam was flummoxed as they left the Town Hall and John explained his dilemma. The solicitor's office was only a short walk away. They entered and John asked for Mr O'Sullivan. 'He is with a client right now, but when he is finished, I will ask if he will see you,' said the receptionist.

Half an hour later, a man came from the office and left the building. The secretary entered and emerged from the office and spoke, 'Mr O'Sullivan will see you now.'

John was apologetic about the disturbance at short notice and explained his fear. The contract was only two pages long and the solicitor read it quietly for a few minutes before saying, 'There are no surprises in there. I know Sam Jenkins; he is an honest man. If you have a successful dairy farm up and running five years from now, you will have fulfilled the contract and the deeds will be passed over to you. Can you fulfil the contract?'

'Yes.'

'Then you have nothing to worry about.'

'Thank you, how much do I owe you?'

'You are starting up a local business. Can I add you to our list of clients?'

'Yes.'

'Then there will be no charge at this stage.'

They re-entered the chamber where they happily signed the contract. Wayne was now present, and they arranged to set off the next morning bright and early.

They set off at six the next morning; it was Saturday a lovely June day with many hours of daylight ahead. Wayne was in the lead on his buggy with two adult family members and a child aboard. The pace was slow, the two mules, well fed and strong as they were, having to pull the heavy waggon with eight people and their baggage as a load.

Chapter Nineteen

They had anticipated that the journey would take about seven hours, but in fact, because of the heavy load the mules needed to be rested every two hours. They travelled southeast from Kingston towards Odessa. The roads were well maintained and even, as they approached Odessa, Wayne took them on a southern road towards the village of Asselstine. The sides of the road were mainly wooded and after an hour, they came to a farm track which led them across pastureland towards Millhaven Creek which they could now see in the distance.

John was in his element. *Perfect for dairy farming, the land has obviously been cleared many years ago by loggers,* he mused. As they approached the Creek, they could see two buildings. 'I see no fences or walls showing the layout of the farm,' he shouted to Wayne.

'Don't worry I have a map with me showing the exact boundaries.'

Half an hour later, they pulled up outside the two buildings. They were surprised to see a beautiful, detached house built of stone and wooden logs in an acre of land which was sewn with potatoes and many other different vegetables, all looking pristine and very well maintained. Stationed outside was a small waggon. Built next to the large vegetable garden in a small compound was an adequate barn, again well-built and sound, with two cows and a horse grazing outside.

'Right,' said Wayne. 'This is my job. I have to serve upon them notice to quit. This won't be easy.'

He began to walk towards the door which opened and a large man holding a rifle stepped out. 'Don't come any closer or I will not be responsible for my actions,' shouted the man who John and Liam assumed to be Jake Morris.

Wayne stopped in his tracks. 'Mister Morris I have been sent by the authorities to serve on you notice to quit this land as you have not fulfilled your obligations...' He stopped talking and moved back as Jake Morris pointed the rifle at him.

Jake was shouting, 'Clear off all of you and take your bullyboys with you. This is my patch and my house you will have to take me and my family out of here in a coffin.'

As the debacle was going on, John and Liam had been taking in the whole scene and conferring, they had reached an agreement.

'Wayne, stand back please,' said John. 'Jake, can we talk man to man. I am not an agent or a policeman or any kind of bullyboy I am a farmer, and we want to start farming this land. I think that we have a solution that will suit us all.'

'I hope that this is not a trick.'

'No trick. Can we talk?'

'You on your own come inside. Madge.' He called to his wife. Still suspicious he said, 'Watch the rest of them while we talk. If any of them move call me.'

Inside, John saw that the house was as well built in as out. Jake indicated a table, they sat at opposite sides and John began, 'Jake I am in the position that you were in five years ago. I must have a dairy farm up and running here in the next five years or I will lose everything. The big difference I think is that I am a farmer, and you are obviously not.'

'I am a joiner and builder I don't know why they put me here in the first place. I only know that I have put my heart and soul into building what you can see and that I am not moving away.'

'I think that we have a solution to both our problems. Can I call Wayne to join us he can help us with the legal side of things?'

Jake was still clearly suspicious. 'Don't forget I have still got this.' Nodding to the rifle in his lap. He called to Madge at the door. 'Madge, will you ask Wayne to join us?'

As Wayne entered John said, 'Please ask Madge to join us too, the people outside are my family, they won't come near unless invited.'

The four sat around the table. Jake and Madge were narrow eyed and uneasy not knowing what was to come.

'Jake, am I correct in saying that there are two hundred and fifty acres of land here?'

Jake nodded.

'And you are only occupying one of them.'

He nodded again.

'Have you any claim on the rest of the land?'

He shook his head and spoke, 'No.'

'Then it is our intention to make you and your family a gift of this house and that acre of land provided that we are able to do so.' He looked at Wayne.

'Yes, I don't see a problem there, you are the owners with the caveat that you understand. You can't sell the land for the next five years but under the circumstances I am certain the council with allow the gift of that small piece for the sake of harmony.'

John looked at Jake and Madge. 'Now that we understand the word caveat, I prefer the word condition, I have one to impose. As part of the deal, you will become our first employees. You know the land and the boundaries; you Jake are also a builder. We have stone masons with us, but they are not joiners or house builders, and we need those skills. We will start to pay you wages once we are up and running. Are you willing to accept those terms?'

The look of relief on the faces of Jake and Madge was palpable. 'Yes,' she said, with tears in her eyes. 'We accept.'

'What about the barn and cows?' said Jake, tentatively.

'The barn and land are ours. The cows are yours and you can graze them on the land for as long as you wish. We need the barn; it will be our home until we can build houses. Are you going to stop nursing that gun now?'

Jake laughed, pointed the rifle at the fireplace and pulled the trigger, there was a click. 'It's not loaded I never intended to shoot anyone.'

The families outside heard the roar of laughter from within. Sarah smiled and spoke, 'It sounds like we have a deal.'

At that time of year the days were long, and they all spent a very pleasant evening together. The mules and Wayne's horse seemed happy to graze alongside the cows. Later the families retired to the upper barn, they made beds by draping blankets over the clean dry straw they found up there, where, after a long and tiring day they slept soundly. Tomorrow would be the beginning of the long process of the creation of a dairy farm. For now, all they required was sleep.

Having rested his horse overnight, Wayne set off for Kingston the following morning in some trepidation. He had said, for the sake of peace that the gift of the house and acre of land to the Morris family would be ratified by the council. Now he began to wonder if that had been a mistake.

Later that day, he walked into the office of Sam Jenkins and put the proposal to him. 'And you said that would be okay?' said Jenkins.

'Yes, have I done wrong?'

Jenkins scowled slightly. 'Had I been there I would have suggested that they allow the Morris family to stay there indefinitely but retain the ownership.' His face lightened and he continued. 'But, on reflection I knew Jake when he worked here for the council, he was a good and loyal worker. That is the reason why he got the land in the first place, our error of judgment is probably why he was in such difficulties. Okay, draw up the deeds in the name of the Morris's and I will sign them.' Wayne walked from the office feeling quite relieved.

That same morning found John Gill walking the extremities of their land with Jake. There were no fences so as they went, they cut branches from the trees and knocked them into the ground at intervals so that John would know where to build fences when the time came.

Liam, Connor, and Paddy busied themselves in the barn sectioning off a third of the area into rooms and creating outside toilets, whilst the ladies made acceptable beds from the clean straw sown together with the canvas stripped from the wagon. For the time being, they cooked on a fire outside.

That evening they sat around their outside fire chatting when Jake reminded them that they were almost into July and before they would have time to build warm houses the winter would be on them, and they had probably never experienced the depth of coldness that would descend. He and Madge would happily take some of them into the house, but there would not be room for all.

'You will all need warm coats. I will take you into Odessa where you can buy them at a reasonable price, and I suggest that you build a fireplace in your living area of the barn for your heat and cooking.'

He told them of a small quarry he had made for his own use in the woods about a half mile away.

That was all the stone masons needed to know and within the next two weeks, a large stone fireplace had been erected and the one third of the barn was fast becoming a comfortable family home ready for the cold, white winter which would descend upon them in November.

While this was going on, John and Jake had fenced off three sides of a large field for grazing cattle, the fourth side being the Creek itself. Another huge field alongside which had not yet been fenced was for the winter hay.

At a mealtime one evening, he announced, 'We are spending money like it's about to go out of fashion, we have bought lots of farming equipment food and clothing and we are starting to run short of cash. We need to start making money. There is a cattle market in Kingston this weekend and Jake, Liam and me are going. I am hoping to buy twenty in calf youngsters and drive them the twenty miles back here, we will be away for a few days. While we are away, I have a task for the rest of you. Field number two. Emily knows which one, the grass needs to be cut, dried, and stored for the winter. There are sharpened scythes, rakes and pitchforks in the barn; Emily and the girls know the drill. Please have it stored away in the hay loft before we return. Thank you.'

Early the next morning, they set off in Jakes small cart leaving the mules and larger waggon for the hay makers. As they travelled together in the cart, John continued to speak of his worries about the remaining money. 'As I understand it, we will pay about twenty Canadian pound for each animal that will not leave us much in the bank. It looks like we will be living frugally this winter. We will be able to start some production this winter as the calves are born, the gestation period for a cow is about nine months. The last one should be born in February or March, so by the spring we will be in reasonable production.'

The rest of the families hooked up the mules and waggon that morning and headed out to the hay field. Only Emily and Madge had seen it before, when it came into view the rest were bemused. 'We are expected to cut and make hay out of all that,' said Connor. 'I am now glad that I am a stone mason.'

'It's only about twenty acres, maybe a little more,' replied Emily. 'Come on let's put our backs into this.'

The next day at the cattle auctions, John was disappointed when he saw the quality of the animals on show. Herefords were the cattle of his choice, and they were there in abundance, but even though fully grown they were small and thin, obviously they had been poorly maintained and fed. He was assured that most were in calf and the prices were considerably less than he had expected. He was still reluctant to make any kind of offer.

As he walked along the cattle pens, he saw something that surprised him, a very handsome, well-built and beautifully proportioned Hereford bull for sale. He approached the salesman. 'Can you tell me who owns that bull?'

'Yes, it's the man in the black shirt over there Frank Skipton.' John approached him. 'Mr Skipton, my name is John Gill and I have recently arrived in Canada, and I am looking to set up a dairy farm. I am looking for twenty Hereford cows in calf. I am disappointed by what I have seen here. I am very impressed by your bull. Do you have any cows for sale?'

'Where is your farm?'

'By the Millhaven Creek twenty miles from here.'

'Do you want to buy the bull?'

'I would if I was ready, but I'm not yet.'

'I farm five miles to the north from here so we will not be rivals. If you follow me tomorrow, I will sell you twenty good quality Herefords, all in calf and in tip top condition, a little more expensive than the ones you see here.'

'How much?'

'Twenty-five per head'

'I'll take them, what time do we go.'

'About eight from here, meet me in the Kings Head at six. I'd like to get to know you.'

They met at six as arranged Frank was seated at a table. Jake and Liam decided to let them talk business, so they stood by the bar and ordered their beer.

'John,' said Frank. 'I bumped into a friend of mine before I came here, he is also acquainted with you. Sam Jenkins. From what he said I have had a change of heart.'

'You mean that you are no longer going to sell me your cattle?'

'No I don't mean that. Sam is very impressed by you and your family, and he has asked me to help you out best I can. I am going to sell them at the normal price of twenty pounds a head. Not only that I am going to throw in a waggon load of turnips to see your animal over the winter. Have you enough hay gathered.'

'It is being stored as we speak. I really don't know what to say other than thanks.'

'I'm thinking that we can help each other out in the future, for instance I don't like to put the same bull to my cattle every year. In breeding can cause many problems as you must know.'

The pair shook hands, seeing that Liam and Jake joined them at the table and the four shared a very enjoyable two hours together.

The next morning, the trio followed Frank to his farm. They were amazed by what they saw, beautifully built farmhouses and barns with fields full of cattle as far as the eye could see. All looking in immaculate condition. Frank took them inside a barn where they could see about fifty young heifers – all looking good!

As John paid for the animals, Frank said, 'Okay, take your pick, do you want to check whether they are in calf or not?'

'Frank. I am very happy to take your word for it. They are all in excellent condition I will take the nearest twenty.'

'Okay. Where you are located your animals should be safe from bears wolves and particularly cougars, they are generally further north. But I would not waste too much time in getting dogs to round up and protect your animals.'

'Thanks for the advice. I will leave them inside at night after milking.'

The three men, now firm friends began the difficult twenty-five mile drove back to Millhaven. At first, Jake took the front position with the cart, hoping that the cattle would simply follow. Liam took the rear to ensure none were left behind and John took a central point to stop the cattle from heading off the track to graze.

'The next time I do this I will have a dog to do the hard work,' shouted John.

They had covered five miles and were just north of Kingston when John again shouted, 'Oh no.' They had reached a small clearing in the trees with a stream and John shouted again, 'Pull them over onto the grass.'

After they had done so, Liam said, 'What is it John?'

'Can you see the way that heifer is holding her tail and the staining around the vulva.'

'I think so.'

'She is about to give birth at any time. It may be in the next few minutes or hours from now, but we can't have her going down on the road, so we may be here for some time. It's my fault I should have checked that none were so far gone.

'We are getting low on food for ourselves, the cattle can graze, will one of you go back into the town and get some human fodder?'

Jake volunteered, Liam and John sat down to wait. Half an hour later, a large waggon came by loaded down with sacks. The driver as he passed shouted, 'Are you the ones from Millhaven Farm?'

'Yes,' replied John. 'This lots for you curtesy of Frank Skipton, anyone need a lift.'

'No thanks we are fine.'

'What are those?' said Liam.

'Turnips.'

'I hate turnips.'

'Don't worry they are not for you.'

It was midday when Jake arrived back with delicious pork pies. As they ate John shouted, 'Did you see that?'

'What?' they both replied slightly startled.

'The water bag just dropped; the birth is upon us.'

Liam watched open mouthed over the next hour as the heifer became a cow, it was late in the afternoon when it was over with, the animal had delivered a healthy female calf and needed no help from anyone.

'Can we go now?'

'Sorry, no, the cow and calf need to bond, and the calf needs to feed. It will be tomorrow morning before we can get going again.'

'Ah well, thank god for pork pies.'

Jake produced a bottle of whiskey and spoke. 'And the water of life.'

Back at the farm, the families were just getting the last of the hay into the barn when the waggon rolled up and the driver announced the delivery of two tons of turnips. Emily and her daughters were aware of their future purpose, and they were stored in the lower part of the barn.

At four the next morning, the drove was underway again with the calf on the back of the waggon and the mother following closely. In fact, the calf appeared to be a beacon for the rest of the heifers as they became less inclined to wander off track and progress was good. So much so that with occasional rest, water, and grazing periods they arrived at

Millhaven Farm in the late evening. The cattle including mother and calf were put into the barn for the night and the men went home for a well-earned rest.

John was still up early the day following the drove; he checked the heifers to see if any other births were imminent which they were not and he re-located mother and calf to the meadow by the barn for their safety and the rest to the nearby field for grazing.

Liam came by and spoke, 'When will you start to milk this cow?'

'Quite soon, in about four or five days. She will produce far too much milk for the calf who will need to be managed on her milk for around four weeks, then she will need to be milked twice a day at least for ten months to a year.'

'Anything you need from me?'

'Glad you asked I was going to ask you to get your building gang together and build a creamery abutting the barn, about forty feet square with an entrance from the barn and to build a stone fireplace back-to-back with the barn so that the butter and cheese makers will not freeze and some warmth will be allowed into the barn for the cattle during the cold months.'

In fact, all the heifers had calved before the years end and John planned to get them all back to a bull which he would hire from Frank Skipton in the very early spring. He saw great potential in one male calf and singled it out for future development.

Thus things, at long last began to go well and as the winter drew in around November time production of milk, butter and cheese were beginning to improve and money from sales started to, quietly but steadily at first, enter their coffers.

Building work had to be discontinued because of the cold and snowy weather and all family members concentrated their efforts on farming until the weather improved.

Spring and summer came at last, and Liam and his team began the building of a large barn and two family houses close to the Creek. A gateway was created with the name Millhaven Farm on it and a driveway to the new houses was completed.

John had bought four dogs, two huge Newfoundland, which he was training to stay with the cattle and guard them during the days grazing and two Border Collies for rounding up the cattle and bringing them to the barn for evening milking and overnight safety. He, with a great deal of assistance, began to fence off more grazing and hay making space.

Later that year, he bought from Frank twenty more in calf heifers.

John, Emily, Liam, Sarah, and their families were able to move into their new beautiful homes.

The third year saw more development with homes for Connor and Emelia, Paddy, Hannah, and Mickey who was now almost five years old.

That year, they had animals for the market, and the milk, butter and cheese businesses were thriving.

Liam, Connor, Paddy and Jake were now ready to start their own business. There was a demand for house building in the Kingston and Odessa areas, as emigrants were moving in all the time. John asked one last favour before they went on their way. He knew that he would miss them and their labour around the farm and he asked that they build a small row of houses near the entrance to the farm in order that he could recruit and house farm hands. They were happy to do so but that took the rest of that year.

The four men were available that year for haymaking and heavy farm work but warned John that they would not be available the next year.

That winter came and did not present any problems. In the spring, John knew that he was going to lose four good men about the farm, so he made it widely known that he was looking to hire farm hands.

In early April the next year the snow had melted, and the warm weather was back. John intended to extend his milk herd to sixty that year. He was working in the barn one afternoon when Emily came to him to announce that three young men had arrived at the farmhouse asking to see him.

They introduced themselves as brothers Sean, Michael, and Peter Shaughnessy from Donegal. They had arrived in Kingston two days before and were looking for work. The three men were in their twenties and looked quite fit. They explained to John and Emily that they had left Ireland because of poor prospects and had paid their way to Kingston where their finances had almost run out. When questioned it seemed that they knew a little about farm work, enough to know that it was physically hard work. They had left their wives and four children in a boarding house in Kingston with the last of their money and had walked from early that morning the twenty miles after hearing that work may be available.

They laughingly said that they had been lost a couple of times on the journey and had eventually found their way more by luck then good management.

'Will your wives be looking for work?'

'For sure yes, they will try anything.'

John took an instant liking to the three. 'Walk with me please,' he said and took them to the newly built small houses near the gate. 'Have a look around,' he spoke.

They did so and when they came back to John, Sean said, 'They are lovely, but we will be a bit cramped all ten of us in one of those.'

John laughed. 'How about one for each family, rent free, all your food found and a small wage on top.'

They could not believe what they were hearing. 'When do we start?'

'Now.'

'But we need to go back to Kingston for our wives and families.'

Emily chipped in, 'That looks like my job.' She turned to John. 'Will you need the mules and waggon for the rest of the day?'

'They're all yours.'

'I'll take Emelia, we can do a bit of shopping while we are there, see you tomorrow.'

'Why am I not surprised?'

That year saw the four builders, with the aid of finances from farming take great steps in their new venture. Jake had been brought in as a full partner, profits going three quarters to the family enterprise and one quarter to Jake. He was the one who knew other builders and people in the area. They opened a small office in Kingston and employed a young woman to take orders for them. In that first year they built three houses, the new owners of which praised them to high heaven so much so that the orders for the next year exceeded their four-man capacity and with Jake's knowledge of the local workforce they began to employ staff.

Chapter Twenty

The fateful year of eighteen fifty-six eventually arrived. The year that because of the legal caveat the deeds to the farm were to be discussed by the Council in Kingston.

Millhaven dairy farm was now the second largest in Upper Canada. Second only in size to the farm owned by Frank Skipton and that was only because it was limited by the land mass. They were now running eighty dairy cattle on the farm. The butter and cheese business had grown enormously, and their products were becoming known and selling well as far away as Toronto. Each year, they were now selling both bullocks and heifers of very high quality in the local markets.

John was now employing six farm hands including the Shaughnessy brothers, all the family ladies were working in various capacities on the farm. He was a benevolent employer and people were happy working with him.

Liam, Connor, Paddy and Jake were now running a thriving house building business with offices in Kingston and Odessa.

Sarah, Hannah, and Madge were the cooks. Hannah, who was now expecting a second child in the next two months took Mickey with her everywhere she went. He was now almost seven years old and as happy as a child could be. There was no school near enough for him to attend, but with the family all around him he did not lack in education.

Emily took charge of the milking and the creamery, and with eighty cows to milk morning and evening, she made certain that everyone played their part including the Shaughnessy ladies, her husband, his farm hands and any of the builders who happened to be around at milking time.

Emelia was also expecting a child around the same time as Hannah, her sisters Mary and Eileen had become engaged to marry two young men from Odessa and were deliriously happy.

The day came, sunny and warm, was it eviction or justice. John and family did not know what would happen that day. They had been given notice to expect a large gathering from Kingston Town Hall at lunchtime, so they prepared a lunch which included much of their own product. John had a few bottles of the water of life handy for commiseration or celebration.

At twelve on the dot, a large carriage arrived and Sam Jenkins together with Wayne Taylor and several Councillors alighted.

The smile on the face of Sam Jenkins did not spell gloom for the families. He held the farm's deeds in his hand and his speech began, 'At the very beginning we had high hopes of you, and you have exceeded everything we hoped for…'

He was a politician, and the speech went on for the best part of an hour. At the conclusion of the speech, John held the deeds of the farm and the future of these united, honest, enterprising and hardworking families was now at long last assured.

Historical Notes

This is a book of fiction, which includes some facts. The period 1845 to 1850 was notorious in Irish history as the time of the great famine. The country at that time was mainly an agricultural society with very little industry. It was part of Britain and controlled from London and by a British appointed administration in Dublin Castle, landowners appeared to rule the roost and the poor, it seems were generally disregarded and had to fend very much for themselves and relied on growing their own crops, particularly potatoes, to survive.

During the time 1845 to 1847, a potato blight struck which devastated one third to a half of the country's potatoes, which turned black and rotted in the ground. This was the straw which caused great suffering and starvation among an already poor and hungry population. Disease became rife, particularly typhus and dysentery, and around one million of the poorest died in a painful and nasty manner.

Around two million people who could see no future for themselves emigrated to England, North America, and Australia.

Most voyages to those countries were unpleasant, but none more so than that of SS Londonderry which set off from

Sligo in November 1848 with one hundred and eighty passengers aboard for a voyage to Liverpool. As it rounded the coast in the north, it ran into a storm.

The captain ordered all the passengers to be squeezed into a hold eighteen feet by twelve. Water began to pour into the hold and a wood and tarpaulin cover was placed over it. The passengers began to suffocate and die.

When the ship called at Derry it was found that seventy-two people had died. Thirty-one women, twenty-three men and eighteen children.

A reporter for the Belfast Newsletter later wrote, 'They lay in heaps, the living, dying and dead. One frightful mass of mingled agony and death, men, women and children…'

St Georges Hall Liverpool was built between 1841 and 1854 when it opened as a Court of Assize and Concert Hall. A magnificent neoclassical building, it served as an Assize Court until 1971 when it became a Crown Court until 1984.

The author well remembers being involved as a CID trainee in a five handed rape case in St Georges Hall in the 1960s, each male defendant had a barrister and their lone female victim had to suffer harsh, intimidating questioning from all five. She was a strong lady and held her nerve, the rapists were eventually convicted and sentenced to long terms of imprisonment.

The three reservoirs Lower Rivington, Upper Rivington and Anglezarke in Lancashire were built by Liverpool Corporation in the years 1847 to 1851. They were built to relieve suffering by the people of Liverpool from the various ailments brought on by drinking filthy water. The chief engineer was Thomas Hawksley. Three hundred various tradesmen were involved; they were generally referred to as navvies. Of these approximately one hundred were Irish.

When these reservoirs were being constructed, a fourth already existed built some years before for the people of Chorley. Some years later a fifth, the Yarrow was built above the Anglezarke reservoir.

Two watermen's cottages were built during the construction described in this book, a third was built some years later at the junction with Horrobin Lane. All three bear the Liver-bird crest of the Liverpool Corporation carved in stone on the front, together with a cross, which appears on the face of it to be a religious symbol, it is not and is in fact a depiction of the tool used to open and close the gravitational flow of water from one reservoir to another.

As you walk along the Street Lane by the reservoir today, you will see two other beautiful cottages, the Gardeners and the Grooms. These were built around the same time as the cottage on Horrobin Lane.

These of course were just more of the fantastic achievements by civil engineers and their workforce throughout the Victorian period of the nineteenth century. Canals, tunnels, railways, bridges, and other constructions built almost entirely by manpower alone.

The Blackrod area adjacent to this build had several coal pits at around this time. In this book, I have referred to the Blackrod colliery disaster, this was a pit explosion in 1836 just a few years before the reservoirs were built, resulting in the deaths of twelve people. Five of the dead were girls, the youngest aged ten years. One of the men who died that day was seventy-two years of age. A few years before this disaster, children as young as eight had been sent to work down the mines. It could be said that this gives us a clue as to the value that the authorities placed on the quality of the lives of poor people at that time.

In England and Ireland, the Poor Laws were in force. Australia, and Canada and other parts of the Empire were eager to accept immigrants to extend their workforce. The cost of evicted tenants and people in the workhouses were a financial burden and a threat particularly to landlords, who saw emigration as a solution to reduce the costly number of destitute people. It was cheaper to send them abroad than to keep them at home. Once on board a ship, their financial burden ended.

During the very long journeys, the passengers were mainly confined to the lower decks which were deeply unsanitary and gave way too much sickness. Burials at sea were a frequent aboard these ships. Those sailing to Canada were forced, during the famine years to stop at Grosse Island Quarantine Station on the St Lawrence River downstream from Quebec, where many were found to be suffering from 'ships fever' which was very probably typhus.

In 1847, many ships mainly from Britain were delayed at the island where eventually more than 5,000 Irish people were buried.

Robert Whyte's book *1847, Famine Ship Diary. The journey of an Irish coffin ship* gives a day-to-day account of one of these journeys.

Upper Canada referred to in this book is now the Province of Ontario. The Canadian pound became the Canadian dollar in 1867 to match the currency of America who were their chief trading partners.

The End

Ingram Content Group UK Ltd.
Milton Keynes UK
UKHW020018010723
424382UK00005B/78